"You Were All Over Me, Miss Dillinger, and I'm Only Human!"

He stood up so quickly that she didn't react until he was right next to her and had pulled her from her stool. "How many men have you enticed with the unspoken promise of delights to come when all you really wanted was another male model?"

"Don't be ridiculous!" She jerked her wrist away but he retained his hold. "Let go of me!" He didn't let go, but pulled her into shocking contact with the hard contours of his chest. She immediately swung her free arm in an arc toward his face, but he caught it in midswing and forced it down to her side.

"How badly do you want me, Lysandra? How much are you willing to give?"

JANET JOYCE

resides in Ohio, happily married to the man who swept her off her feet as a college coed; she admits that her own romance is what prompted her writing career. She and her family like camping, traveling and are avid fans of college football. She is an accomplished pianist, enjoys composing her own lyrics and reads voraciously, especially the romances she loves.

Dear Reader:

SILHOUETTE DESIRE is an exciting new line of contemporary romances from Silhouette Books. During the past year, many Silhouette readers have written in telling us what other types of stories they'd like to read from Silhouette, and we've kept these comments and suggestions in mind in developing SILHOUETTE DESIRE.

DESIREs feature all of the elements you like to see in a romance, plus a more sensual, provocative story. So if you want to experience all the excitement, passion and joy of falling in love, then SILHOUETTE DESIRE is for you.

I hope you enjoy this book and all the wonderful stories to come from SILHOUETTE DESIRE. I'd appreciate any thoughts you'd like to share with us on new SILHOUETTE DESIRE, and I invite you to write to us at the address below:

Karen Solem
Editor-in-Chief
Silhouette Books
P.O. Box 769
New York, N.Y. 10019

JANET JOYCE
Man Of Glory

Silhouette Desire
Published by Silhouette Books New York
America's Publisher of Contemporary Romance

Other Silhouette Books by Janet Joyce

Winter Lady
Man of the House

SILHOUETTE BOOKS, a Division of Simon & Schuster, Inc.
1230 Avenue of the Americas, New York, N.Y. 10020

Copyright © 1983 by Janet Bieber & Joyce Thies

Distributed by Pocket Books

ISBN: 0-671-47381-6

First Silhouette Books printing November, 1983

10 9 8 7 6 5 4 3 2 1

America's Publisher of Contemporary Romance

Printed in the U.S.A.

1

Lysandra Dillinger came out of her self-imposed fog when a glass of white wine was pressed into her hand. She gave a slight shake of her head, tipping back her slender neck until the silken strands of her long black hair no longer hid the faraway expression in her brown eyes. "Sorry, Sonja," she apologized to her aggrieved-looking hostess. "I was lost in thought."

Sonja Parker gave an affronted snort. "I don't know why I keep inviting you to my parties, Lys. You don't even try to have a good time." Getting little response, Sonja took another tack. "There are some extremely wealthy art collectors here tonight. If you'd mingle a bit, you might find more of your work being displayed in their homes. I've dropped your name right and left all evening."

Seeing the reluctant flicker of interest in Lysandra's eyes, she gently coaxed, "Come on, I've heard a few of these people admit that your life studies come as a refreshing relief. Personally, I think some of the avant-garde works that achieve such critical acclaim look like so much plumbing welded together." Placing her arm around Lysandra's delicate shoulders, she leaned closer and added, sotto voce, "And *that's* supposed to be serious art."

Lysandra giggled. "Loyalty, thy name is Sonja."

"Nonsense." Sonja dismissed Lysandra's statement. "I really feel that way and so do other people here tonight. Of course, a lot of them are still under the outrageously misguided notion that L. Scott Dillinger is a man." She pointed to a man who was seated upon a nearby couch. "For instance, Stanley, over there, feels certain that only another big strong male could depict such power and motion in beasts. I heard him inform his wife that you were a hermit type who lives alone in the Catskills." Sonja's warm laughter erupted.

Lysandra shook her head and took a quick sip of her wine. "I'd love to know who started that rumor." Shrugging, she continued, "Then again, maybe it's best to let everyone go on thinking I'm some kind of recluse." Her voice held a slightly bitter tinge when she continued, "Being thought of as an eccentric mountain man has helped to pay the rent."

A sympathetic frown marred Sonja's impeccably made-up features as she detected the flicker of pain in the eyes of the woman who stood at her side. Though Lysandra tried to hide her dissatisfaction,

Sonja knew that her young protégée disliked being classified strictly as a talented portrait and folk artist by most critics, even if they readily admitted she was a commercially successful one. Lysandra yearned for her work to be taken seriously.

As if she were able to read Sonja's mind, Lysandra quipped dismissively, "Starving in some cold garret was never high on my list." A distracted expression appeared on her face and, without realizing it, she removed herself from the chattering crowd to a quiet place inside her mind.

"Hey! Come back to me," Sonja prodded her humorously. When she was satisfied that she had Lysandra's full attention once again, she asked, "Have you settled on a subject for the piece you're doing for the Bernard-Wilcox show? That may be your big chance to break out and lift a few eyebrows."

The sculpture Lysandra was working on was practically all she had thought about for weeks, and she searched unsuccessfully for the right words to describe the elusive image she was trying to capture. "I know what I want to do, but it's just not working—though I will say it'll be entirely different from anything else I've ever done."

With a look of mock horror, Sonja exclaimed, "Surely you're not going to set a blow torch to a pile of scrap metal!"

Lysandra's throaty laughter was joined by Sonja's delighted giggle. Wearing a shimmering turquoise silk caftan whose swirling print was as compellingly vibrant as her personality, Sonja stood, Junoesque and fair, beside Lysandra, a petite brunette. Lysandra's simple black chiffon highlighted the ivory perfection of her skin and enhanced the mysterious depths of her delicately slanted dark eyes. Her pointed and varied-length skirt allowed tantalizing glimpses of her shapely legs, and the fitted bodice lovingly molded her rounded breasts, tiny waist and slender hips. The two women stood out in the crowd, a stunning picture in contrasts, unaware of the many appreciative glances directed their way.

Clasping her long fingers together, Lysandra admitted, "I'll never go quite that far, but this piece will be something of a departure for me. I'm thinking about doing a complete male figure. I need a model, but so far I've found no one that even comes close to what I want. I'm totally frustrated at the moment and that's why I'm here. I needed to get my mind off my work and be with other people tonight."

Knowing Lysandra too well to be insulted by her guileless admission, Sonja's blue eyes twinkled. "Then let's go find some, shall we?" An amused smile tilted her lips as she watched Lysandra take a fortifying sip of her wine.

"Ready to mingle," Lysandra announced and followed Sonja as they wove their way through the crowd.

"You must meet Todd Bertrum," Sonja declared, pointing to a man seated at the bar. "Bertrum Studio, you know."

Lysandra gave a resigned nod, knowing that Sonja would somehow make sure she met all the "right" people whether she wanted to or not. Despite everything, Lysandra considered Sonja a very dear friend. They had met several years before during an art festival in the Village where, along with other struggling young artists, Lysandra had been displaying some of her work. The figure of a young girl, carved in alabaster and modeled after a child Lysandra had seen playing in a nearby park, had turned out to be Sonja's youngest daughter, Suzanne.

Amazed that Lysandra had captured her daughter's face right down to the tiny impish dimple that dotted Suzanne's left cheek below her eye, Sonja had offered an outlandish price for the piece, which Lysandra had refused, insisting that it go for her original price. Then Sonja's ebullient appreciation of her work had prompted Lysandra to offer it to her as a gift. However, the tall blonde had insisted on paying for it, saying that Lysandra would be foolish to part with any of her work at less than a fair price. Of course, Sonja's idea of fair and Lysandra's had been two entirely different things. By the end of their first meeting a compromise had been reached and Lysandra's rent worries were no longer a pressing concern. Moreover, after that, owning a bust of a loved one done by L. Scott Dillinger had become the "in" thing among Sonja's wide circle of friends. Before Lysandra had been able to grasp what had happened to her, her work was being shown in several galleries, and her financial worries had become a thing of the past.

Lysandra's uncanny ability to bring life and motion to her creations, whether the medium be terracotta, wood or bronze, had pleased her increasingly longer list of patrons, and recently her wildlife studies had even brought a few welcome comments from the art critics. Even though she wished such judgments didn't matter to her, Lysandra had memorized one of their more flattering observations. "Dillinger has proved that there is still a place for naturalism in the arts. Expressiveness of form will forever be the final criterion, popular thought or no."

With the financial security brought by her commissioned work, Lysandra could now afford to support her less lucrative endeavors. At the moment her schedule was such that she felt free to devote herself totally to the elusive image she felt compelled to capture in clay. The figure in her mind's eye was an example of glorious human perfection, both timeless and ageless. She had labeled her idea *Man of Glory,* but the pad and a half of sketches she had compiled were still not clear enough to enable her to start work. Each was missing some essential element she had yet to define. She could describe his features during the day, but they changed in the nightly dreams that had lately become a regular occurrence. In the morning, she would wake up dissatisfied with her previous day's work and have to start all over again.

Lysandra's thoughts were forced back to the present as she and Sonja were waylaid in their progress toward the bar by an imposing society matron. She had to admire Sonja's ability to gracefully extricate them from a lengthy diversion. Sonja's vivacious smile lit her face as she issued a witty comment, then politely moved on, taking Lysandra's arm and drawing her along.

They finally reached the group of people clustered around the huge Victorian mahogany sideboard, which had been cleverly converted into a large bar.

Placing a hand at the small of Lysandra's back, Sonja unobtrusively pushed her into the center of the gathering. With practiced flair, Sonja exchanged effusive greetings with her guests, offering a smooth cheek to one after another of her male acquaintances.

As usual, Lysandra took artistic note of the proceedings. How could she capture in her work that particular flattery men made to women with their eyes? Some of them crinkled their lids and narrowed their eyes to gleaming slits, others lifted their brows then dropped their lashes to express silent compliments. It would be difficult to trap such movement in clay. She forced her mind off her work and back to the man Sonja was introducing to her.

Todd Bertrum was tall, thin and appeared to be in his late forties. A casual smile curved his wide mouth and when Lysandra extended her hand, the contact was firm but brief.

"Todd owns the Bertrum Studio," Sonja explained pointedly, in case Lysandra had missed the information the first time around, while Todd sipped his drink and watched Lysandra with sherry-brown eyes. When she merely nodded at the information, he set down his drink.

"You're not some starving artist looking for space

to show your work?" he asked, his brows lifting in mild surprise.

"No." Lysandra grinned and seated herself on the bar stool he offered her. "I eat quite regularly now." She eyed his confusion and shook her head at Sonja. "Do you do this to him often?"

"Whenever possible," Sonja admitted with a wide smile and absolutely no shame. "Todd has enough money to keep his gallery open even if he hardly sold anything. It's a hobby to him. He asked me to supply him with up-and-coming young talent who need only a place to show and an audience in order to take off." With a wicked wink, Sonja added, "I do my best."

"The supply far exceeds the demand." Todd shrank away from Sonja's mock slap and gave her a salute with his glass as she was called away by her husband, James, to welcome some late arrivals. Todd returned his attention to Lysandra, his expression resigned. "Know Sonja well?"

"She helped launch my career," Lysandra answered distractedly as she fought the impulse to reach out and touch the unusual slant of Todd's nose. It was almost the perfect angle for the man she intended to portray in her next piece. Light would catch the plane and provide the effect she wanted. Her fingers tingled with the urge to explore it tactilely. If she could just feel it, she would probably be able to transfer that particular shape to the clay.

A possible solution to her problem with her next piece came to her as she continued to study Todd's nose. Maybe she could take a feature from every male that fulfilled one part of the image she carried in her brain, then mold them into the clay one by one to form the perfect figure she was striving for. Her dark brown eyes became a shade darker as she noted the shadows beside the slightly flaring nostrils and the tapered cartilage at the bridge.

"Looking for warts?" Todd finally broke into her thoughts, his attractive face split in an amused grin.

She laughed, embarrassed at being caught in the act. "I'm sorry. I'm afraid I was working. You see your nose is almost the one I'm looking for." When his eyebrow rose, she explained, "I'm a sculptor, and I'm having trouble with my latest project. I can see him, but I can't get him to come out in the clay."

"Dillinger . . ." Todd made the connection between Lysandra and the surname unobtrusively inscribed on all her work. "You're not *that* Dillinger?"

"I'm not?" Lysandra answered, amused. She was familiar now with this disbelieving reaction. No one immediately accepted that she was the artist whose fluid pieces depicting animals in motion were becoming more and more popular with collectors. She was too young, too attractive . . . she was a woman!

"But—but, he . . . Dillinger's a man!" Todd stumbled on with a stunned expression on his face. ". . . Isn't he?"

"Lysandra Scott Dillinger." She held out her hand. "It's such a long name, it just seemed simpler to use an initial for my first name. My friends call me Lys."

He shook her hand for the second time with a fast pumping motion that made her laugh. He noticed what he was doing, and a deep red crept above his crisp collar and suffused his face. "Good Lord, I'm behaving like an idiot."

"I'm sure that it's usually the other way around. You have a fine gallery, Todd. I've spent many quiet hours enjoying the works you display there." In a further attempt to relieve his embarrassment, she asked, "How many starving young artists have you met tonight?"

"Too many to count," Todd admitted, relaxing under Lysandra's good-natured remarks. "I don't like to push, but I'm doing a show of naturalistic sculpture in a few months. I'd certainly like to add a few Dillinger pieces."

Lysandra was not surprised to learn that Todd was a shrewd businessman. It hadn't taken him long to get past his embarrassment and take advantage of their meeting. He was aware that her work was drawing increasingly larger crowds and that his gallery would profit from a showing.

"I'd like that, Todd. Right now, I'm involved in doing something a bit different for the Bernard-Wilcox show, but I'd be glad to borrow back from their owners some of the things I've done and loan them to you for your showing. I have a few pieces I could sell in my studio, but I won't have time to produce anything new until the Bernard-Wilcox show is over."

Todd was pleased with her offer, and they began talking like they were old friends. Lysandra found him easygoing and felt herself relaxing in his company. They exchanged anecdotes about the art world and discovered that they shared many of the same tastes. Soon they found they had to raise their voices to be heard as the hired band began to play dance music. Eventually, she and Todd were forced to give up talking, and they swiveled on their stools to watch the dancers who were gyrating around the parquet floor to the beat.

When Todd asked her to dance, she refused gently, saying she would much rather watch. She smiled encouragingly at him when a lovely young woman in glittering purple toreador pants came up and pulled him onto the floor. Giving her a less than apologetic grin, Todd took the woman's hand and disappeared into the crowd of dancers. The people in the room seemed to blur into a rush of color as they moved to the driving beat of the popular music.

Lysandra's gaze strayed across the room toward the floor-to-ceiling windows where the skyline of Manhattan glittered and blinked with multicolored lights. She stared vacantly at the panoramic scene, feeling a bit out of her element and experiencing a sudden longing for the serenity of her studio apartment. She had almost made up her mind to make her excuses to Sonja and leave when a tall man walked into her line of vision and stood with his back to the crowd, looking out the windows at the twinkling city lights.

At first, she was struck by his height and automatically began to artistically assess his body—about six two or three, wide-shouldered with long legs. A shaft of light from the strobes struck his hair, and her breath caught in her throat.

Silver and gold—the same color as the man in her dreams! The light moved away, but her eyes remained fixed on the man. She was too far away to be certain that she hadn't made a mistake, that the light had only given him the illusion of having the exact hair color she re-created every night inside her head.

She slid off the stool and began walking across the room, never taking her eyes off the tall, silent figure as she moved through the crowd. Coming closer, she noted the movement of his shoulder when he brought up his hand to rub the skin above the white collar of his shirt, as if something had prickled the nape of his neck. She wanted to run and grab his hand so she could examine it before he dropped it back to his side, but that would look ridiculous, so she continued her slow approach, savoring the sleek lines of his body without hurry. So far everything about him resembled her image of *Man of Glory*. Judging him to be in his early thirties, he was a fully developed male in his prime.

He was wearing a black evening jacket that was tapered at the waist and dark trousers that hugged his long legs perfectly. She realized he had turned around, but she was too busy researching his body to notice whether he was aware of her approach or not. She was simply grateful that she now had the opportunity to view his chest and smiled when he slid one hand into the pocket of his trousers, enabling her to discern the outline of his hip and thigh where the coat was pushed aside by his arm.

She didn't realize that she had stopped moving

toward him as her eyes traveled up the flat belly to the buttons of his vest, then higher to the brown column of his throat that was mostly hidden by a constricting white collar and elegant black satin bow tie. Everything about him seemed right, but she couldn't be sure unless he removed his shirt or at least unbuttoned it. At the startling mental image of him removing his clothes, she reminded herself where they were. This was a party, not a sitting in her studio! Still, the temptation to do a little more research was too great. She knew she had promised herself not to think of her work at the party, but she couldn't resist inspecting the face that belonged to this magnificent body. There could be no harm in just looking—and besides his face might turn out to be a total disappointment.

It wasn't. Beginning with his chin, chiseled and slightly stubborn with a faint cleft, her eyes took careful inventory. Perfect! His chin was perfect! She let out her breath in an unconsciously pleased murmur, unaware that she was well within earshot.

Taking another step forward, her eyes settled on his lips, molded and firm with a sensual fullness to the lower one that suddenly disappeared when he drew it into his mouth. She didn't wait for him to release it before her eyes moved on to his nose. The nose was even better than Todd's and fit her requirements exactly, with the precise plane, the perfect tilt. The intense feeling that, at last, she had found the right model for *Man of Glory* increased as she lingered over the ruggedly bold features supercharged with an inner vitality that provided what had always been lacking in each of her sketches.

She looked directly into his eyes, and her only reaction to the blaze of blue that stared steadily back into her own was to blink once, then wish there was some way she could portray their marvelous color in her work. Deep in thought, she inwardly acknowledged that she had never seen more distinctive eyes in her life. Sky blue irises were surrounded by deeper violet rings that gave him an exciting, untamed look. She felt as if she were staring at a man who had dressed in modern-day clothes in order to conceal his uncivilized nature—primitive man adorned in the trappings of society that could not completely hide the elemental perfection of their wearer.

"You're perfect," she whispered to herself and knew that she couldn't lose him, that she had to find a way to make him model for her. She gave him a brilliant smile, and when he held his arms open to her, she immediately accepted his silent invitation to dance.

They began swaying to the slow music swelling around them, but Lysandra was oblivious to how well they moved together. Her brain was whirling with the plans his presence inspired. She couldn't believe she had found him after such a short search, that she was actually touching him. His image would never escape her again. If he would only agree to pose for her she would be able to capture him for eternity in bronze.

If the piece turned out as well as she hoped, she

would have exactly what she needed for the Bernard-Wilcox show. She would surprise the critics with a breakout piece of sculpture that would earn her the respect she wanted without having to discard the principles that had so far classified her as a category sculptor.

2

〰〰〰〰〰〰〰

Caught up in the excitement of her discovery, Lysandra wasn't thinking about anything else when she lifted her hand to touch her partner's face, memorizing the lean line of his jaw. The rough texture made her fingertips itch with tactile curiosity, and her hand traveled to his neck of its own volition, then gently curved down to one wide and powerful shoulder. She was annoyed that the hard muscles she felt were covered by the crisp material of his jacket and wondered what he would think if he knew she would have preferred seeing him without the elegant jacket and dark trousers.

As the music came to an end, the jarring noise of people clapping broke into her reverie. She suddenly realized that he wouldn't have to read her thoughts in order to reach some terribly wrong conclusions. Her actions had more than likely done that for her already. What must he be thinking? What else could he think but that she was a woman looking for something far different than a few clinical modeling sessions in a well-lit studio? That supposition was confirmed when he didn't join in with the applause, his fingers remaining locked behind her back slightly below her waist. Although the music had stopped, his hands moved in a slow rhythmic pattern, sliding dangerously lower and lower. Nervously, she broke free of his arms and looked up warily at the roguish male face gazing down at her, the incredibly blue eyes hazy with sensual intent.

One brow was lifted questioningly, his lips curved in a smile that was both knowing and pleased and touched with a bit of worldly cynicism that was completely out of sync with her imagined perception of what he should be like.

"I'd like to talk with you privately for a moment," Lysandra stated in what she hoped was a matter-of-fact tone. "Can we find a quieter place?"

He was wearing the expectant expression of a man who was being offered an unanticipated romantic interlude. She realized she'd given him good reason to think that she was ready to hop into bed with him and had to do something to negate that impression. "I need to talk to you," she repeated.

"Are words really necessary?" he asked finally in a voice that was low and husky, a rich timbered voice that matched the very masculine appearance of its owner. Taking a step closer, he slid one hand around her waist and pulled her against him, his eyes caressing her mouth, her throat, then sliding to her full breasts. A shiver of unwelcome sensual awareness tickled up her spine, and a small frown creased her forehead as she jerked away.

"I would like to make you a business proposition, Mr. . . . Mr. . . ." She realized that she didn't know his name and cursed her impetuousness that only seemed to surface where her work was concerned. Normally cautious when meeting people, she had rushed into this situation without laying any groundwork.

For a second he looked totally taken aback by her words, then he gave her a barely imperceptible nod and took a firm grasp on her arm. "I think I spotted another room off this one that should serve. I think it best if we dispense with names for the moment, don't you?"

She detected a tinge of ice in his tone and from the overtight grip of his fingers on her elbow, she gathered that he was none too pleased by her sudden change of mood. Prepared to while away a few pleasurable hours with a willing woman, he obviously didn't like how she'd taken the wind out of his romantic sails. Perhaps now he wouldn't agree to model for her, but somehow she'd have to find a way to convince him. He wouldn't even tell her his name, which she thought a bit churlish on his part. It seemed as if he wanted to wait until he discovered what was in it for him before giving out any personal information. Perhaps he was the type of man that gave false names to his bedmates so there would not be recriminations from them if he discarded them the next morning. Glancing at the implacable set of his jaw, she realized she might have some difficulty disabusing him of his notion of what was forthcoming.

He remained silent as they sidestepped through the crowd, until he had guided her through a double door that led into the Parkers' study. She had barely stepped inside when he pushed the door firmly shut behind them and pulled her into his arms. Crushed against his chest, her hands trapped between their bodies, her eyes flew to his face.

"Let's see how much you're worth, honey," he growled bending his head to cover her startled lips with his hard mouth. The kiss was brief, savage and accompanied by a rough exploration of her feminine curves with his roving hands. When he'd finished his appraisal, he released his hold and stepped away as if he'd suddenly felt repelled. "You've got a great body, lady, but lousy technique."

Shock and fear drained all color from her face as Lysandra backed away from him. Frantically, she searched for some physical barrier to place between them while his eyes ruthlessly stalked her, increasing her trepidation. She fled behind the nearest couch, her hands clutching the leather upholstery as she stammered tremulously, "Come . . . come any closer, and I'll scream."

He laughed humorlessly, the short harsh sound

assaulting her senses. "You're obviously new at this. You'd better expect to be pawed if you want to make any money in this game. Who the hell let you in here anyway?"

He folded his arms across his chest and leaned back against the door, his stance implying that she was his prisoner until he got an answer to his question. Left in no doubt about his misjudgment of her occupation, anger replaced Lysandra's fright. "I was invited, you dolt!"

Another humorless laugh added further insult. "Not by Sonja or James. I'll keep your little game to myself, honey, but for you, this party's over."

"What?" Lysandra exclaimed. He might look like her *Man of Glory,* but he wasn't high on a pedestal in the intelligence department. "You're making one big mistake, mister, and I'll be happy to set you straight. I came in here to hire *you*—not the other way around." Angrily, she returned the challenging hostility in the narrowed blue eyes that were focused on her face.

His jaw worked but no words came, and Lysandra saw that he had leaped to the wrong conclusions again. She'd never seen a man so angry that he couldn't speak, and she swiftly completed her explanation—anything to bring an end to the stunned silence that stretched between them. "I wanted to hire you as a life model." She paused and pointedly arched a brow before introducing herself. "I'm Lysandra Dillinger. L. Scott Dillinger. I'm a—"

"The sculptor?" If she thought she had shocked him before, he looked totally astonished now.

"You're the one who did *Golden Stallion* for the Myer Gallery's Summer Show?"

"I am," she confirmed.

"I thought you were a . . ." His voice trailed off, and his molded lips twisted in self-derision.

"A what?" she probed antagonistically, tossing her head and lifting her chin, but her wide mouth was curving up at the corners, and her brown eyes were dancing with amusement as they judged the degree of his discomfort. As far as she was concerned, the punishment he'd delivered for her unthinking behavior on the dance floor went far beyond the crime, and she couldn't help wanting to prolong his embarrassment over the truth.

He hid the slight tinge of pink that crept along his lean jaw by turning his back on her. He raked a hand through his hair, giving a slight shake of his head as he said grittily, "A high-class hustler with the brass tacks to crash an exclusive party." Turning back to her, he said, "I apologize, Ms. Dillinger."

Lysandra's smile widened, her temper soothed by the rueful expression on his face. Relenting, she said, "Apology accepted, Mr. . . ."

"Honour's the name. Adam Honour."

Large brown eyes narrowed on his face. "It's not," she negated. "That would be too perfect." He looked taken aback while her mind raced with the meaning of his name. It was just too great a coincidence, and she was unsuccessfully trying to stifle her incredulous laughter when she became aware that he was eyeing her doubtfully, confused by her amusement.

"I was given that name at birth," he announced coolly. "Up until this moment, no one has thought it particularly funny."

Realizing that her laughter had offended him, Lysandra quickly explained, telling him of her idea for her next piece of sculpture. She realized she wasn't making much sense because she was beginning to stammer under the relentless probing of his blue eyes.

When she came to a breathless halt, he gave an indulgent shrug of his broad shoulders and said rather scornfully, "So that's why you were so interested in my body on the dance floor."

A fiery blush rose in her ivory cheeks. "It . . . it really had nothing to do with you personally," she admitted. "I'm sorry you misunderstood."

"Who does it concern, then, if not me?" he asked in an icy tone that held an underlying edge she could not identify. Her apology was completely ignored.

"I have a professional interest in your body—nothing more," she announced reasonably.

His hawkish scrutiny made her uncomfortable, and a small shiver of apprehension prickled up her spine. The real-life *Man of Glory* used his wild blue eyes to dissect and decipher, to ask questions she didn't intend to answer. She lowered her gaze, forced a bland smile on her face and moved to the front of the couch. Sitting down, she attempted to quell the trembling in her legs by crossing her ankles and folding her hands in her lap.

"Now that you know I'm a sculptor," she began, hoping to get back to the subject uppermost in her mind, "maybe you can understand. You fill my needs perfectly, right down to your name. I want you to model for me, and I'm willing to pay well for your services. This particular piece has been on my mind for weeks, and it means a great deal to me."

"I'd like to see where you work."

His sudden switch to a new topic threw her for a second, but then she gave him one of her rare smiles of genuine pleasure. He was going to take her up on her offer, she was almost sure of it. "When?" she asked softly, somewhat mesmerized by the intensity of his gaze.

"Now," he returned bluntly, walking to where she was seated and offering her his hand. "I'm leaving town tomorrow, so if you want to continue this sales pitch, it'll have to be tonight. I never agree to anything without checking out the facts."

"Certainly," she agreed swiftly, not considering that she was rashly allowing a total stranger to come home with her, someone who had manhandled her only moments before. He didn't allow her a moment to think but pounced on her affirmative answer and swiftly acted upon it by drawing her up from the couch.

The feel of his strong hand guiding her through the crowded room as they went to find Sonja and James set off a series of danger signals within her. She had told him what she had thought was the truth when she said she had no personal interest in him, but his warm touch was doing odd things to her equilibrium.

Sonja was too involved with her other guests to make much of their early departure, but Lysandra didn't miss the delighted gleam in her hostess's eye as Adam dropped her wrap over her shoulders and tucked her arm possessively under his as they turned toward the door. Their fast exit was halted briefly while Adam and James exchanged a few words.

Forty minutes later, Lysandra inserted her key in the lock of her studio apartment in the Village and led Adam inside. While she moved to turn on the lights and hang up her wrap, she could sense that he was silently studying the room.

Pieces of wood and clay were scattered across the floor immediately surrounding her workbench, which occupied a prominent location in the center of the room, directly beneath the skylight. During the day the overhead light was immensely important to her, but she was suddenly aware that, at night, the moon cast a romantic silver glow across the whole room. It bathed the space with pale light and shone like a spotlight on the turntable, highlighting the mound of clay covered with clear plastic sheeting.

One wall was lined with shelves that stored shellac, wax polish, scrim, brass fencing and soap. Her tools hung neatly on the wall: hammer, saw, pliers, wire cutters and drills. A set of boxwood modeling tools lay on a side table, cluttered with polythene bowls and a series of blunt chisels. Large sketches of her various subjects were pinned to the walls, and his assessing eyes missed nothing.

She stood just inside the door and watched him walk through the studio, picking up a tool, examining a finished piece of her work with knowing fingers, then replacing it exactly where he found it. When his gaze strayed to the small daybed that occupied that corner of the room designated as her sleeping area and lingered there too long, she became aware of the vulnerability of her position.

"This is where you sleep?" he asked, lifting her worn flannel robe off the bed. Casting her a mocking smile, he let the robe fall from his fingers. "Is this all there is?"

"There's a small kitchen out there," she said and pointed to the folding doors on the other side of the room and was annoyed when he walked over and disappeared through them as if he had every right to inspect her private space. He was back in a few seconds and moved to the large windows, toying with the chain of a large potted fern hanging from the ceiling. "Do you like horses?" he inquired, spotting the bronze stallion that stood on a small pedestal nearby.

She relaxed enough to smile at him. There wasn't a trace of mockery in his voice, and that question was often asked because so much of her work involved horses. "Yes, I do. I enjoy riding, but I haven't done much since I was a child."

She sat down in a rattan chair, expecting him to join her in the living area she had arranged on a Persian rug in front of the windows. Instead, he remained where he was, concentrating on the bronze stallion. "That's not for sale," she said gently. She held her breath. Many people had tried to get her to part with that particular piece, but for some reason she found that she couldn't bear to sell it. The stallion had come alive for her in her dreams, its powerful body flying through the haunted passages of her sleep, disturbing her, exhilarating her, almost as much as the unnerving man who now stood admiring it did.

She had once done another similar sculpture, but it had taken another form, a tamer version that didn't reveal the passion she had depicted in the first. The savagely pounding hooves had been softened, and the wild flare of nostrils had been erased. The gentler work had been presented as *Golden Stallion* and had been sold to a Colorado rancher not long after it had been exhibited. Mr. Myer had been told by the buyer that the horse looked remarkably like a favorite stallion he used for breeding purposes on his ranch. She had never met the buyer but sometimes mused on whether or not he would be better pleased with this more savage rendition of the powerful animal.

In a moment of honesty, she realized that the emotions that had exploded to the surface and been culminated in the pawing stallion had frightened her. Those same emotions were surfacing once again because of Adam. Half of her wanted to retreat behind the barriers of self-protection she had erected around herself, but the other half yearned to release her real feelings, not only in her sculpture, but in a relationship with a man.

Could she open herself to that kind of vulnerability? Emotional involvement brought pain, and she didn't want to experience such agony ever again. No, she would make sure that she kept Adam Honour safely categorized in her mind simply as a useful body. She needed his challenging looks and inherent vitality to bring life to her next sculptured image, but she wouldn't fall prey to them as a woman.

Her favorite subjects had always been animals and children—safe subjects that still expressed motion, vulnerability, pride—but like her bronze stallion, her next work was going to be a departure for her. All she had to do was convince Adam to help her make *Man of Glory* a reality. She wished she could convey to him how necessary he was to this piece, to express the inner need that was compelling her to do it.

When Adam turned to face her, his features were curiously tight. "You really are L. Scott Dillinger, aren't you?" he asked as if he wished it weren't true.

She wasn't surprised that he hadn't believed her without the additional proof. Her behavior tonight had been provocative, but she was sure his doubts had gone beyond that. Because she rarely appeared at her showings, having little taste for the accompanying notoriety, a ridiculous mystique had built up around her, and most people believed she was an eccentric old man. "Lysandra Dillinger," she affirmed, watching him closely as he ran his fingers over the molded flanks of the bronze horse.

She was having difficulty keeping her eyes off him, partly because he was a vastly interesting subject, but partly, she had to admit, because he had the compelling good looks few women could ignore. Attempting to camouflage her interest, she stood up and walked over to the table, then sat down on the nearby stool, keeping her face averted.

She was fascinated by him, both as an artist and as a woman, but the woman would have to be denied. She had already noted that his moods changed constantly, his strong features and turbulent blue eyes reflected emotions as mercurial as the weather. She wanted to witness them all, to assimilate every nuance of form, every shade of expression. He had a spectacular body. He could also read her mind.

"In the nude?" His drawling question seemed to bounce off the stark walls.

She jumped. "What?"

"Do you want me to pose in the nude?"

Displaying a very nonprofessional blush she hoped wouldn't give him the wrong idea, she strove for a casual tone. "Certainly." Feeling that she sounded a bit more defensive than she would have liked and needing to cover her increasing nervousness, she began toying with the damp clay on the turntable in front of her. She needed time to gain more control of herself, so she switched the subject. "Were you surprised to find out I'm a woman?"

"A beautiful young woman who blushes like a schoolgirl?" Adam said, mockingly. "Yes, definitely." He took a chair on the other side of the table and sat, stretching his long legs out in front of him.

Lysandra couldn't withstand the urge to explore the male limbs lying so enticingly close, unaware that she was asking for trouble. Her gaze traveled from ankle to thigh, wishing she could see through his trousers to the corded leg muscles she imagined beneath.

"And surprised that she didn't have the guts to ask

for what she wanted right out from the beginning."
He retaliated with an appraisal of his own. The
purple rings around his irises melted into the blue as
he visually caressed the delicate bones of her oval
face, the graceful column of her throat and the
breathless motion of her full breasts beneath the
black silk of her bodice.

Adam didn't hide his reaction to her, showing her
with his appreciative glance that he liked what he
saw, but Lysandra ignored the invitation in his eyes
and doggedly pursued the original subject. "If I'd just
walked up to you and asked you to model for me,
would you've agreed?" she questioned caustically,
giving the clay a vicious stab with a wire-ended
tool, which marred an entire hour of work and sent
the turntable spinning.

"Probably not," he said, snarling. "But you didn't
do that, did you? As far as I could tell, you had only
one thing on your mind."

"That's true," she retorted. "My work!"

"That's not what it felt like, Ms. Dillinger. How was
I to know you were casting me as a marble statue?"

"Bronze," she shot back, her temper rising as his
erupted to the surface. She supposed his ego had
taken a blow, but he hadn't shown it at the time, and
she had to set him straight as quickly as possible.
"And you didn't seem to mind."

"What man would? You were all over me—I'm
only human!" He stood up so quickly that she didn't
react until he was right next to her and had pulled
her from her stool. "How many other men have you
led on when all you really wanted was a model?"

"Don't be ridiculous!" She jerked her wrist away, but he retained his hold. "Let go of me!" He didn't let go but pulled her into abrupt contact with the hard contours of his chest. She immediately swung her free arm in an arc toward his face, but he caught it in midswing and forced it down to her side.

"How badly do you want me, Lysandra? How much are you willing to give?" He smiled down at her furious face, slowly bringing her closer with a firm pressure applied to her spine.

"I don't want *you* at all," she insisted, reeling with the knowledge of her helplessness. His eyes were glittering with unknown emotions, his muscles were like tempered steel against her softness as he deliberately leaned her back to the table and his rock-hard thighs pressed intimately against her legs. "I thought I'd apologized for how I behaved, but if not, I do now." Lysandra tried to sound calm, but when she felt his breath near her cheek she burst out, "Do you need a pound of flesh as well?" Her brown eyes were ensnared by his hypnotic gaze, and his mouth twisted in a sardonic grin as he captured her wrists with one hand, then lifted her chin with the other.

"One kiss, Lysandra," he murmured seductively, watching closely for her reaction. "You can consider it another clinical notation for your sculpture."

Before she could speak, his lips brushed gently across her open mouth, making her lips tingle. She pressed them together tightly to stop the pleasurable sensations, but he laughed at her mutiny. She could feel his silent chuckles vibrating inside his chest as clearly as she felt every muscle along the entire length of his body.

He was not aroused, merely playing with her, intent on getting some response out of her. His tongue traced the outline of her mouth, and she gasped in protest. Immediately, he took advantage of her lapse, confiscating her lips and delving between them. His expertise was devastating as he explored and enticed, seeking a reaction she was finally incapable of denying him.

She tasted him with the thirst of long abstinence, breathed in the wholly male scent that only made her more aware of his undeniable virility and gave herself up to his kiss. Dizzy with a newly awakened desire that had captured her unawares, she clung to the hard male body pressed against her. She had no idea when his hand released her wrists or that she was clinging to him eagerly, her arms wrapped about his neck.

His warm mouth lifted, and his caressing breath dried the moisture on her flaming lips. "That was for L. Scott Dillinger, but this is for me."

Before lowering his lips again, he tangled his fingers in her long, silken hair, pulling her head back far enough for her to see his eyes. Seconds before she had sensed his detachment, but now she saw the exact opposite. The violet rings that reminded her of a wild animal flooded the blue, and his eyes became twin prisms of flashing indigo lights. The cynical grooves beside his mouth had disappeared and were replaced by a lazy half-smile. The silvered light from

35

the window above cast entrancing shadows across his sculptured cheekbones, making him look exactly like the elusive image she had dreamed of so often. Further thought was impossible when his mouth enveloped hers, infusing a new depth of passion even greater than what she had experienced before.

He claimed everything, her lips, her tongue, the tender inside of her mouth until she no longer felt they were her own, but his, for as long as he took pleasure in them. Her feeling of deprivation when his mouth moved on swiftly turned to trembling fulfillment as his lips followed the line of her jaw to her ear, nibbling the soft lobe until shivers raced up her spine.

In a dreamlike stupor, Lysandra succumbed to the pleasurable fantasy of being caressed by the all-male creation she had conjured up in her mind. She had pictured this man too often, admired his perfection too long to be able to withstand this assault on her senses. Her murmurs of delight were for the phantom male she had conceived weeks before.

In a euphoric haze, her fingers winnowed through the silver gold strands that feathered back from his temples. Turning her face toward the corded column of her neck, she trailed soft kisses upward to his jaw, savoring the rough texture of his skin. Her active participation incited an aggressive response in him that swiftly jolted her out of her fantasy world. She was kissing a real man who, unlike the passive male in her dreams, responded to her slightest touch. She felt the slight tremor that ran through his body before he wrapped her closer in his arms, his hands splaying over her rounded buttocks and pushing her hips into the cradle of his own. The intimate contact with his arousal made her realize she was far out of her depth. She attempted to pull back, but by arching away from him, she exposed her throat, and Adam slid his lips downward, tantalizing the soft flesh with the tip of his tongue.

"I knew you'd taste like this," he breathed. "Feel like this." His fingers worked beneath the wide straps of her dress, easing them off her shoulders until the black material slipped away to reveal the white curves of her breasts. He branded heated kisses along the quivering pearly flesh, using his fingers to mark each spot his lips touched, restaking each claim his mouth made.

"I can do much more for you than pose, Lysandra," he drawled huskily. "Admit you want me." The arrogant demand lifted the last shred of enchantment shrouding her.

Using every ounce of willpower she possessed, she twisted in his arms. "No," she cried, pushing against his chest. She captured his face with her hands, forcing him to stop the tantalizing torture across her breasts. "This never should have happened." Her words were shaky, more a whisper than the sharp pronouncement she intended.

Immediately, he broke off the embrace and stepped back, roughly pushing back the straps of her dress. "You enjoyed it. Every minute of it," he stated harshly, the violet rings no longer muted but focused on her with startling clarity.

Unable to hide the trembling in her soft lower lip,

still swollen from his possession, she stared back at him, her eyes dark and luminous. "You went too far," she declared tremulously, shaken by how close she'd come to ending up in bed with him.

His scornful amusement was obvious. "No," he bit out. "But I did even the score. Now you're aware I'm a man, not just a model."

She was far too upset to be angry. It had been months since she'd felt desire for a man and even then she had felt nothing like this. He had no idea how deeply he had "scored." They were not even, not on any level. He had successfully knocked apart the fantasy world she had built up around him, and her dream man faded away to be replaced by the living Adam Honour. She had to say something, had to go on as if nothing had changed, when in reality everything had changed completely.

She doubted she could look at him with clinical abstraction ever again. He was indeed a man, and she had responded to him like a woman who passionately wanted him. She couldn't let him discover that the kiss went far deeper than his calculated retribution had intended. She made a superhuman effort and looked up at him. "Now will you agree to model for me?"

His pupils contracted dangerously before he stepped away from her. "We'll discuss that later." He pointed to her kitchen. "Do you have anything to eat in there? I'm starving."

"I . . . I have eggs." She ate so irregularly when she was working that she could scarcely remember what her fridge contained, and she was hardly in any shape to cook.

Dazedly, she watched him walk through into the kitchen, heard him rummaging in her cupboards, then he called back to her that he'd make them both an omelet if she wanted to go fix her face. Startled, she looked across the room to the mirror fixed on the wardrobe door and angrily saw why he had offered the suggestion.

Her black hair lay in tangles about her face, the dark strands contrasting sharply with the alabaster paleness of her cheeks. Smudges of mascara marred the translucent skin beneath her brown eyes, and her mouth looked bruised. Shattered by her tousled reflection, she quickly went to make the necessary repairs.

3

~~~~~~~~~~~~~~~~~

Lysandra and Adam ate silently at the small rectangular table that occupied one corner of her kitchen. Adam could barely fit his long legs beneath the table, and when he had brought the perfectly cooked cheese omelet from the stove, he had to duck in order to keep from striking his head on the Tiffany-shaded lamp hanging from the ceiling.

Toying nervously with the food on her plate, Lysandra tried to decide if she could separate her personal feelings for Adam from her professional needs. He had blasted through her defenses and aroused emotions within her that she wasn't sure she was prepared to deal with. But it was the flesh-and-blood Adam, with his elemental maleness and inherent strength, who was necessary to bring *Man of Glory* to life. Those exact qualities had been missing in her sketches, and it was that realization that became the deciding factor. She wouldn't allow her personal fears to jeopardize her work.

"Will you pose for me?" she inquired hesitantly.

He had an odd expression on his face that gave her the impression he would have liked to evade her question, and he answered her with a question of his own. "Do you have to work here?"

"This is my studio. All my supplies are here," she replied. "Is your job the problem or what?"

"That bronze horse in the other room . . ."

"I told you I won't part with it," she interrupted, assuming he was trying to arrange for compensation in advance.

"I once had one of your horses." He grinned at her astonished face and nodded. "I bought *Golden Stallion* because I thought it was an accurate replica of a horse we used to have. You captured Hurricane very well in that piece, but his true personality is better portrayed by that bronze in the other room. We bred a fine line of horses from old Hurricane."

Adam's voice grew husky. "That animal was my father's pride. I gave him the bronze, and he cherished it until it was stolen, along with several other things. I came to New York to commission you to do another to give my father for his birthday. I'm prepared to pay whatever you ask for a new one, but I thought since you already have another . . ." He paused and fixed her with an intent gaze. "I might pose for you if you let me have that bronze."

"No," she blurted, then seeing the barbed glance he threw her, held up her hand. "I'm sorry that your father's sculpture was stolen, but I . . . I won't sell mine."

She wouldn't admit that the bronze revealed too much about herself, things she didn't care for anyone else to see. She deeply regretted that Adam had already seen it and hoped he wouldn't delve into the emotions that had inspired it. Few people were aware of her turbulent childhood. She didn't want anyone's pity, so she stubbornly kept the painful memories to herself—memories of uncaring strangers in foster homes that sheltered her for a few months at a time but never gave her any sense of permanence. The young woman who had been her mother had never returned to claim her, and it was still very painful to recall the day she had heard one of her foster parents call her an illegitimate misfit who was better suited to her dream world than the real one.

Too shy to make many friends, she had developed a great affinity for animals and had spent many long hours sketching them, observing them, depicting them in clay, so she had something to hold that would be hers. Now she worked with bronze because it was the most permanent material she could find—all she created would endure.

"It could be recast, couldn't it?" Adam's question brought an abrupt end to her recollections.

Shaking her head to dispense the last of her tormenting memories, she spoke softly. "Usually the mold has to be chipped off in pieces, but even if it was intact, I would have destroyed it. I don't believe in copies. Each piece takes something from me that I'm only willing to give away once."

"I want that bronze." It was a threat. "If you won't sell, I won't model."

"But that's totally unfair!" she fumed. "Your modeling fee won't even come close to what I would get for that if I sold it in a gallery." She was going to stand up, then thought better of it, intimidated by his expression.

"And you want to do *Man of Glory* very badly." His smile was predatory. "You've made that point very clear. It gives me a great deal of leverage, and I plan to use it to my advantage." The clear cut of his jaw was pronounced, the soft firmness of his mouth unrelenting. It was difficult to ignore the flashing demand in eyes that seemed to bore into her soul.

"You don't understand anything." Brown eyes battled with blue. "All I need are a few sittings, maybe some photos. I can do most of the work from memory." She tried to outstare him, but seconds later he forced her capitulation.

"If you come to my ranch and work there, I'll pose for no fee, and I'll commission you to do another horse."

"Why would I do that?" she asked, but they both knew she was considering his offer. The compulsion to do almost anything to ensure that he would be her model was great.

"Why not? I'll provide everything you need. We have a room not unlike your studio where you can work."

"But that's crazy," she insisted. "I'll only need you for a week at the most. Carting all my supplies and equipment across the country seems a bit foolish when you could pose for me here, starting tomorrow, and accomplish the same thing."

"I'm leaving New York tomorrow morning." He raked one hand through his blond hair, and Lysandra frowned at the implacable set to his chin and the slight tinge of pink along his jaw. "Look!" he snapped impatiently. "You might find this hard to believe, but I won't take my clothes off for you unless we do it in my own home where I'll be assured of total privacy."

Her brows rose incredulously, and her eyes glittered merrily at his discomfiture. "You mean it would bother you to pose in the nude? You don't seem the kind of man to have a modest bone in your body."

"You won't see what kind of bones I've got unless you come to my ranch. That's the deal. Take it or leave it."

She recoiled from the irate edge to his voice as he went on. "And, dammit, you don't know one thing about the kind of man I am."

"I know you're one of the most stubborn men I've ever met," she berated him. "And I could accomplish everything I need with you without flying off to Colorado. I could lock the door, and we would have perfect privacy right here."

His fierce scowl was answer enough, but she couldn't resist punishing him for forcing her hand. "I hope the rest of your body is worth all the trouble I'm taking to see it." Deliberately, she ran her eyes down the taut lines of his trousers as he angrily rose to his feet, but when she looked up to see how he was taking her challenge he was grinning at her. It was a wide flashing show of white teeth, almost a leer, but his eyes gleamed with genuine amusement.

"So you accept?"

"Yes," she snapped, exasperated by his ability to throw curves. "But I'll only stay as long as I need you to model. Then you transport everything I bring out there back home, and you'll pay a fair price for commissioning my work." When his smile didn't slip a centimeter, she threatened, "And I won't begin work on another horse for your father until I finish *Man of Glory.*"

"Agreed." He made it sound like a major victory for him, and she was ready to hit him. Did he really have to be in Colorado now, and was he actually that modest—or was there some other reason for his demand that she travel to his home? When he coolly sauntered out of the kitchen with her following behind like some well-trained dog, her hands bunched into fists. He told her to have whatever she needed packed and ready to go by the following afternoon—which, he added, was already a postponement of his scheduled departure. Waiting for her reaction, he leaned nonchalantly against the door, crossing his arms over his chest. He didn't have long to wait.

"There is no way I could be ready to leave by tomorrow! I'll make my own travel arrangements and wire you the time of my arrival."

"Tomorrow or never, Lysandra." His tone was

unrelenting and backed up by the penetrating blue of his eyes. "My ranch is well off the beaten track. You can't expect me to drop my affairs and come pick you up whenever you call. My time is valuable, and you're lucky I'm being as generous as I am."

Feeling as if she were being manipulated by a professional, she tried still another approach. "Then postpone going back for another day. Nothing can be so important it can't be put off for twenty-four hours."

His shoulders came off the wood frame and in seconds he had placed himself before her, intimidating her with both his height and his nearness.

"My business in New York was finished this afternoon," he informed her bluntly. "I'm giving you the morning to get ready and even that's far more time than I have to spare. Perhaps when you get to know me better you'll understand I have little other choice. There are people depending on me back home, and I won't let them down in order to make time for something they wouldn't understand in a blue moon."

"What won't they understand?" Lysandra asked, even though she sensed his growing frustration with the conversation.

"Stripping down to my birthday suit for the sake of art will seem mighty strange to the people I know. You're asking me to do something that I won't find easy to live down. As far as I'm concerned, I'm giving you one hell of a lot for what I'm getting in return. I can almost hear the jokes starting now."

Stung and offended by his words that implied he thought modeling for her was beneath his dignity, she retorted, "Some of the finest art in the world depicts the nude body, and you'll have every reason to be proud when I complete *Man of Glory*."

"Will I?" He sounded highly skeptical. "What do you plan to do with the piece when it's done? Show it off to the world or keep it next to that bronze horse for your own private enjoyment?" He gestured toward the gleaming statue standing across the room. "I don't mind you handling it, but I'm not thrilled with the idea of being 'exposed,' so to speak, to the world."

"I thought that kind of thinking went out with Queen Victoria." Lysandra was becoming angrier and angrier. "No one will know it's you. I'm presenting it at the Bernard-Wilcox show, and those who attend are much too sophisticated to wonder about the model."

"*I'll* know it's me," he said. "And I'm not so sure those sophisticated art lovers share your lofty sentiments."

"Are you going to do it or not?" Lysandra inquired, tossing her long black hair over her shoulder as she defiantly faced him.

"Are you coming with me tomorrow or not?" Adam countered in a similar tone.

"All right!"

"Fine." He glibly accepted her compliance and swiftly moved to the door, pulling it open and stepping out into the hall before turning back to her.

"A deal's a deal. We leave tomorrow from La Guardia. I'll rent a van and be here by noon to load up whatever you need." He left, smiling.

She was certain she could hear him whistling down the hall after he had closed the door on her infuriated face and couldn't dispel the sensation that more had been decided than business arrangements.

What had she let herself in for? She couldn't fly off to Colorado without knowing a lot more about the man, and there was no way she could gather more information. Then she recalled his friendship with the Parkers. Perhaps Sonja could give her some facts about the audacious rancher from Colorado who had arrived on the scene like a blowing tumbleweed and was planning to roll her along with him out of town. Even though it was late, she walked to the phone and dialed Sonja's number, hoping the party was over and her friend could talk.

4

A very unsophisticated whoop of laughter echoed over the phone as Sonja Parker exclaimed, "Adam Honour is going to pose for *Man of Glory?*"

"Yes," Lysandra admitted hesitantly. She had tried to sound businesslike when describing the recent turn of events, but Sonja wasn't buying it.

"You lucky girl! I've thought that man glorious from the first time I laid eyes on him and have trouble remembering that I'm a happily married lady with children every time James invites him to our apartment."

"Sonja!"

"Let me get this straight," Sonja continued, having a difficult time controlling her amusement. "No hot romance but a strictly business arrangement?"

"That's right," Lysandra reiterated weakly, remembering her own reaction to Adam's kiss and the feel of his body pressed to hers. "And I was wondering if you could give me some background information. Mr. Honour hasn't told me very much about himself, and for a good portrayal, I need to know more. Besides, if I'm flying to Colorado, I'd like to know what I'm getting into."

Lysandra was grateful when Sonja shelved her attempt at matchmaking and became matter-of-fact. "Adam belongs to his valley and his ranch and that's about all I can tell you. He and James were at college together and kept in touch because Adam wanted a good broker in New York. We visited his spread a few years ago. I must say that I enjoyed it immensely. It's beautiful in a rugged sort of way. The few times I've been with him, Adam was always very friendly and quite good company." She paused before slipping back into character, and said "And Lys—there's no Mrs. Adam Honour."

For some reason Lysandra hadn't even thought of that possibility before Sonja brought it up. She wanted to ask for more information but was afraid that Sonja would think she was attracted to Adam— and she didn't feel prepared to answer any pointed questions.

"Well, thank you, Sonja. I wish I didn't have to go all the way out there, but it was the only way he'd agree to pose for me."

As Sonja bid her good-bye, Lysandra sensed that the woman was about to fall on the floor laughing— which certainly didn't help her peace of mind. "What have I done?" she asked aloud after hanging up the phone, but she was too afraid to contemplate the answer.

Adam arrived at her studio promptly at twelve the next day. He eyed the packed crates stacked neatly by the door, looking very surprised that she hadn't changed her mind during the night. "You really do want to sculpt me, don't you?"

"I think I made that clear last night," she asserted, trying to keep composed when he shrugged his wide shoulders out of his casual sportscoat and handed it to her. She draped the navy blazer, still warm from his body, over her arm, resisting the temptation to stroke the fabric. She was unable to keep her eyes from following him as he turned away. The untamed part of him that had been thinly disguised by his elegant evening clothes was now overwhelmingly evident. His well-developed biceps and powerful forearms lightly hazed by golden hair were tanned to a deep brown. His Rugby shirt stretched across massive pectorals then tapered in, molding to his narrow waist. Well-worn jeans embraced his long legs and clung to his lean hips to disclose every virile line.

Looking down at her luggage, Adam said, "This is less than I expected." He glanced back over his shoulder and at that moment wished he could take Lysandra into his arms and kiss her as he'd wanted to as soon as he'd arrived. But, for now, he had to step carefully, he reminded himself. He was both intrigued and challenged by the half-wary, half-provocative expression in her soft brown eyes, eyes so large they dominated her small face. Their delicate slant fascinated him and added to the air of mystery that surrounded her. When she'd floated across the room into his arms last night, all seductive woman, he'd felt an overwhelming desire, and she'd yet to convince him she hadn't felt it, too. He'd sensed that he could have persuaded her into bed, but when he took her, he didn't want her to have any reservations. He needed more time to convince her that she desired him as much as he desired her, and the only way he could buy that time was to take her home with him.

The dramatic change in her appearance this morning amused him, for she was obviously trying to prove that, today, she intended to be all business. He could tell by the upswept arrangement of her dark hair, the crisp linen skirt and pristine blouse that she intended to hold herself aloof. But it wouldn't be long before she was on his home ground, and once there he was sure he could break through her cool stance.

Matching her businesslike attitude, he advised, "Make sure you take a jacket. It'll be late afternoon by the time we land, and it's usually chilly. We're close to the mountains and, even in July, it cools off early."

"Do you realize what transporting this cargo will cost?" she said, knowing that her attempts to dissuade him from his projected course of action were doomed to failure.

"It's my plane, and I carry what I want," he

replied, casually dismissing her testy question and bent to pick up a crate. He lifted it easily up on one shoulder. She was so busy admiring the play of muscles along his tensed shoulders that she didn't hear his question, and he had to repeat it. "Have you flown in a small plane before?"

"You *are* a qualified pilot, aren't you?" she asked a bit shakily.

"Afraid of flying, too?" he inquired without turning around as he marched out the door.

"What do you mean, too?" she called, picking up her large suitcase and following him down the stairs of her building and out to the van. When he had deposited the first crate and her suitcase in the back, he started back for another load. She was behind him every step of the way. "Well?" she demanded breathlessly at the top of the stairs.

"Last night you were afraid of ending up in bed with me, today you're afraid of taking off in my plane." Without any show of strain he lifted another heavy crate onto his shoulder while she digested his words.

She waited until they were heading toward the airport before speaking to him again, trying to convince herself that she was doing the right thing in accompanying him to Colorado when she knew that it was probably a grave mistake and something she would regret for a very long time. She had to find a way to put things back on a professional basis and squash his repeated attempts to bring sex into their relationship.

"I'm not afraid of flying," she stated coolly. "But

53

I've no way of knowing whether you've got the right qualifications." She paused, then added pointedly, "And I wasn't interested in ending up in bed with you for the same reasons."

"Is that so?" He laughed softly. "Trust me, Lysandra, I've gotten high marks in both flying and lovemaking. Give me a little more time, and I'll prove it."

She stiffened in her seat. He was outrageous! She fixed him with a deadly stare that had little effect—he remained cheerfully alive and still kicking.

"What a coward you are."

"What?" Her indignant screech made him grin, deepening the grooves that lined his cheeks.

"I know the difference between an artist at work and a woman on the make." He increased speed and swerved in and out of the traffic with the superb control of a race car driver. "Do your models have to pass some kind of test before you take them to bed?"

"Listen," she demanded irately, "I want you for *Man of Glory* and nothing else! Let's get that clear from the beginning."

"So you say, but I think it goes deeper than that. However, I'm willing to wait and give you proof of my qualifications at another time." He gave her a quick glance from his side of the van. "Maybe later when I strip for you."

Lysandra's stomach plummeted, and she swallowed convulsively. Whatever had made her think she could put this man in a safe place with a few insults?

He reached across the seat and patted her lightly

above the knee, smiling tenderly when she jerked her whole body away from his touch and tried to meld herself into the door. The man was more than she could handle, and she was a fool for agreeing to this ridiculous setup.

"You can turn this van around, Mr. Honour. I am a serious artist, and this trip was supposed to be strictly business." She tried to sound cold, but felt as if she were being kidnapped by some ancient Viking who was abducting her to some distant land to lay claim to her body. "I'm not going anywhere with you. Our deal is off."

"Hardly," he remarked casually, returning his attention to the lane changes he needed to exit for the airport. While his attention was seemingly diverted, she decided that as soon as they reached their destination she'd jump out and call herself a taxi.

Again he read her mind. "Coming with me is the only way to get your sculpture done," he reminded her, then added, "We're both adults. I know that you want me as much as I want you, but if you want time to rationalize those feelings, it's okay by me. I'd only want you if you were willing," he said with a mocking look that was guaranteed to annoy.

"Well I'm not willing, so you won't have me!"

"We'll see. . . ." His eyes made a quick survey of her body, but it was slow enough to note the rapid rise and fall of her breasts.

Fighting to keep from squirming, she said between gritted teeth, "This is a mistake." He had parked the van in the short-term parking lot and rolled down the window to speak to two young men who had obviously been waiting for his arrival. Adam handed one of them the keys to the van, then got out and exchanged a few more words with them. Then he walked around to her side of the van and helped her out. He kept a firm grasp on her arm as they walked across the taxi-lined intersection in front of the terminal. "I don't want to go with you," she said, trying again as she practically had to run in order to keep up with his long-legged stride. "This is crazy . . . it's . . . I feel like I'm being kidnapped."

"Come now," he said and laughed, but lengthened his stride, rapidly covering the distance down the ramp to the gates that led to the planes, "we have a verbal agreement, and I'm simply holding you to it."

Maybe she could free herself from the firm grip he had on her arm when they walked through airport security, she thought quickly. She gave him a narrowed glance as he dropped her arm so she could pass through the square arches first.

The flashing lights and blaring alarm shattered her composure completely, and she jumped out of the other side like a shot. "What the—" she exclaimed as she was instantly flanked by an airport security guard on one side and a female attendant on the other. She had to stand still while they passed a metal detector over her figure, and she was stunned after she was told to empty her pockets to find a metal money clip in her blazer's left pocket. The airport personnel apologized to her for the inconvenience, and Adam's arm was back on her elbow the very next second.

"Shall we go?" He nodded politely to the attendants and prodded Lysandra along.

"You planted that on me!" she accused as he dragged her down the congested hallway.

"Saved time. We're late as it is, and I need to get home. I could have talked you out of all the second thoughts you're having, but this was quicker. Try not to put such sinister connotations on everything I do." He dropped her elbow and took her hand, giving it a gentle squeeze. "I suppose all you artists have overactive imaginations."

"That was a lousy trick," she insisted, feeling no less threatened than before. His hold on her hand was playing havoc with her senses. She knew she wanted to go with him but didn't want him to know what she was thinking.

They reached the gate and it no longer mattered; the decision to stay behind was taken out of her hands. She was ushered firmly through the gate into a waiting six-passenger Falcon, which must have cost the earth. Astonished by the plane's plush interior, she barely noticed when Adam solicitously buckled her into her seat but bristled when he slid into the seat beside her. "So you're not the pilot!" She gave him a withering look that only brought a slight quirk to his lips.

"Never said I was, only that I was qualified." He pointed to the front of the plane where the two men from the parking ramp were settling themselves into the first and second seats. "Bob and Paul work on the ranch, but part of their jobs are to cart me around the country. Bob's the best pilot we have, and Paul is our C.P.A. You'll find that most of us have to wear several hats."

While she digested that information, the small plane taxied onto the runway and was given permission to lift off. With little other choice, she relaxed in her seat and prepared herself for the long flight ahead of them. After a while, when the panorama of skyscrapers below them passed out of sight, Adam carefully steered the conversation on to innocuous subjects that put her at ease in his company.

"Lysandra is a lot of name for such a little woman. Is that what everyone calls you?"

"No. Most people call me Lys."

He repeated the shortened version of the name she had always felt was far too ostentatious. It rolled off his tongue like a breathless caress. "Lys. I like that. Different, just like you." He unbuckled his seat belt and rotated his seat toward her. "Have you always wanted to be a sculptor or some kind of artist? I know very little about you except that you're a beautiful woman who wants me to take off my clothes." His smile was maddening, and Lysandra was equally annoyed at the color that she could feel rising in her cheeks. "I don't even know how old you are. There's such an aura of innocence and unreality about you, I don't know if you're a well-developed minor or an ageless Grecian priestess."

"Now who's not dealing with reality?" She laughed. "I'm neither. I'm twenty-eight years old and have been on my own since I was eighteen." Not giving him the chance to ask why she had been independent so young, she rapidly continued, quickly telling him that she had always sketched and played with clay. "I worked my way through art school and managed to land a scholarship after the first year that helped keep me there. Like most, I struggled for a while, and I'm just beginning to become successful."

Not satisfied with such a brief explanation, Adam delved further, wanting to know about the jobs she had had during her school years and everything about her past. After an hour, she realized that even though she hadn't offered any details of her childhood, she had told him nearly everything else there was to know. Surprised at how relaxed she now felt in his company, she described how she'd developed the concept for her next work, which she hoped would depict man as he was meant to be—the alpha and omega of creation.

"I think you fit your name almost as well as I do mine." Adam chuckled. Seeing her blank expression, he explained, "In Greek history, Lysander was the one who freed the souls of men from the mundane things of earth. Considering what you want to do with me, I don't know if I should be flattered or scared to death. I've never thought about man in that way before."

"Now you understand why I want to do this piece," Lysandra stated, musing over the meaning of her name as she stared out the window. "I want to show the inherent beauty in man that has never been lost since the beginning of time. Every bone in your body was once there in the first Adam, every muscle made for perfect efficiency of movement—

your face could have been his face. I hope to show man in his glory and to remind the world that mankind was created above everything else on earth."

When she turned to look at him, feeling a bit embarrassed at how much she had revealed of her emotional involvement with her work, she couldn't tell what he was thinking. There was nothing mocking in his expression, nothing to indicate that he thought her a foolish romantic, but something between them had suddenly changed. If she didn't know better she would have thought he looked distraught, but she had no idea what part of her speech might have upset him.

"You'll have to forgive me, Lys." Adam pulled down a portable table in front of his seat. "I have a lot of paperwork to go over before we touch down. There are some magazines you can leaf through or perhaps you'd just like to catch some of the scenery out the window."

Confused by the shuttered look that came over his rugged features, Lysandra said, "Of course. I'm sorry if I've kept you from your work." She turned her head away to stare sightlessly back out the window, was startled when he took her hand.

"I'm glad you explained a bit about yourself, Lys." He gave her hand a gentle squeeze, then released it in order to unclasp the catches of his leather briefcase. "I didn't mean to cut you off, but duty calls." He lifted a stack of papers onto the small table, and Lysandra reacted to his apologetic expression with an answering smile.

"I never realized a rancher would be inundated with paperwork," she admitted. "Do you have a large ranch?"

"You'll see soon enough," he informed her shortly, but softened the cryptic remark by saying, "I'll take you riding and show you my land. However, if I want to have time to do that, I've got to go over some of these figures."

Soothed by his offer to take her horseback riding, she nodded and pointedly picked up one of the magazines he had mentioned before. "Get to work," she prodded when she realized that his eyes were still on her. "I'm holding you to that ride. It's been years, but I can't wait to get back up on a horse."

A companionable silence fell between them, and it wasn't much longer afterwards that Lysandra began to nod. She had stayed up most of the night to complete her packing and was exhausted. She nestled her head against the back of the richly upholstered seat, and her eyes closed.

5

~~~~~~~~~~

Long-fingered shadows were forming at the base of the mountains, but the peaks were still bathed in gold as the gleaming silver plane touched down and sped across the tarmac. The jet engines whined down, and there was complete silence as Lysandra gazed in awe at the sweeping green valley rimmed by darkly wooded foothills and snow-capped peaks.

Adam had gently nudged her to wakefulness when they flew over the Rocky Mountains, which rose in jagged splendor toward the sun. When he saw her delighted response to the rugged beauty displayed through the window, he'd grinned and remarked that the best view was yet to come. "In the morning, you'll really see the 'purple mountain majesties' in all their glory."

Accustomed to the gentle slopes of the eastern

mountains, having never been beyond the Mississippi River, Lysandra had not been adequately prepared for her first view of the Rockies. She couldn't think of words to describe them, and she wondered how the first travelers who had come upon them must have felt. She could only imagine the sense of shock those early explorers would have experienced on first viewing the awesome mountain range. After weeks and months of trudging across the flat plains, what must they have thought when they began to see the distant peaks rising on the horizon? She had been prepared by pictures and films, but even so those lofty images paled in comparison with such magnificence viewed firsthand.

She tore her eyes from the breathtaking view of the valley through the plane's window when she felt Adam's fingers in her lap unbuckling her seat belt. "Your eyes are almost as wide as your mouth," he teased. "Let's get out of this plane and into that clean mountain air."

He grasped both her hands and pulled her up out of her seat. Strong arms enveloped her and pulled her closer as Lysandra turned her bemused face up toward his. She started to ask him the distance to the ranch house when his mouth descended, and his lips fastened around hers as he gathered her against his wide chest. Surprise immobilized her as his tongue glided along her lower lip and entered her mouth where he playfully encircled the moist cavern. "Welcome to the Bar H," he breathed huskily before releasing her and turning away, almost as abruptly as he had pulled her into his arms.

A spreading warmth pervaded Lysandra's body just as it had done the evening before when Adam had kissed her at her studio. What was there about this man that turned her into a malleable lump of clay? He had made no intimate gestures during the flight, barely touching her during the hours they had shared. She had gradually relaxed in his company after the earlier suggestive remarks he had made at the airport had almost caused her to cancel the trip. She'd talked herself into believing that his sole reason for inviting her to the ranch was so that she would create another bronze horse to present to his father for his birthday.

Shakily, she followed his broad shoulders out of the plane and down the steps. Striding ahead of her, he waved at the bouncing pickup truck that was rapidly moving toward them. The vehicle came to a sudden halt, mere inches from Adam's tall figure, and a large silver-haired man jumped out. He clasped Adam briskly on the shoulder, and the two men exchanged a few words that Lysandra couldn't hear before Adam turned his attention to her.

Stretching a long arm toward her, Adam indicated that he wanted her to meet the older man standing beside him. She crossed the yards that separated them, all the while feeling two pairs of similarly intense blue eyes studying her every feature. The closer she came, the clearer it was that the older man had to be Adam's father. Introductions were made, and Lysandra's deduction was confirmed.

Clayton Honour clasped her small hand within his two large calloused palms. "Welcome to Colorado and the Bar H, Miss Dillinger. This is indeed a surprise and a pleasure. I had no idea that the creator of *Golden Stallion* was a dainty little gal like you." Clayton's tanned face was wreathed with smiles, and his blue-eyed gaze was friendly. He was nearly as tall and broad-shouldered as his son, but the years had softened the uncompromising lines of his chin and face. Whereas Adam's blue eyes had the discomforting effect of seeing into Lysandra's soul and continually shattering her composure, Clayton Honour's blue eyes were warm and comforting.

She smiled and voiced her pleasure at being in Colorado and her growing appreciation for the beauty of the land. Clayton's silvered head bobbed and his pleased smile broadened, bringing into greater prominence the weathered lines about his eyes.

"Most folks react like that the first time they see the big rocks. Some are even a mite scared by the sheer size of 'em, but I can see that you're a lady who can appreciate them and not be frightened off." He took her arm and helped her into the truck while Adam placed their luggage in the back.

Moments later, Lysandra found herself wedged between the two broad-shouldered men in the front seat. The elder Honour had insisted on driving and suggested that his son point out the landmarks they were passing as he concentrated on the winding roadway that led up the foothills of the mountains. Adam's arm was stretched across the back of the seat, and his hand was firmly planted on her shoulder, effectively keeping her pressed to his side. The tantalizing movement of the long fingers of his left hand etched patterns through her clothing to the heated flesh of her shoulder, making her increasingly uneasy. She tried to unobtrusively shrug away from his touch, but although he ceased the movement of his fingers, he kept a firm grasp on her shoulder. That he was aware of her discomfort was apparent by the glint in his eyes when she glanced up at his face.

His gaze took a meandering path across her reddening cheeks and came to rest on the rapid rise and fall of her breasts as her breathing increased with her agitation. He knew exactly what he was doing, and he was embarrassing her in front of his father. Clayton Honour would have to be extremely gullible if he went on believing that Adam had invited Lysandra to the ranch for any other reason than to share his bed.

Did Adam frequently import women for lengthy stays at the ranch? Clayton had mentioned something about always enjoying Adam's friends' visits when they had been introduced. Surely a man like Clayton Honour, whose gentlemanly courtesy and demeanor implied that his sense of morality was identical to his last name, wouldn't condone Adam's openly flaunting his bed partners?

There was something very honest and forthright about Clayton Honour. He was a man as rugged as the mountains where he made his home, but the warmth that emanated from his lined, leathery face bespoke a gentleness and an old-world respect toward women. Hoping he wasn't getting the wrong impression of her, Lysandra tried with little success to concentrate on the breathtaking scenery they were passing through.

Spruce trees covered the hillsides on either side of the road, which wound continually upward until it reached a plateau where nature had created a large open meadow. Clayton slowed the truck almost to a stop when Lysandra gasped at the view.

Nestled snugly in the middle of the protected meadow was a sprawling split-log ranch house. Native stone formed the lower half of the walls and supported the heavy logs that completed the structure. Natural cedar shakes, silvered by the sun, covered the inviting home. A split-rail fence enclosed the front yard of the house and wandered further to delineate the rear paddocks where several sleek horses stood grazing. Beyond these were distant pastures with stocky Hereford cattle, enclosed by more modern fencing of barbed wire. It was a picture of pastoral beauty.

Clayton smiled broadly when Lysandra exclaimed, "It's beautiful!" It was so peaceful looking that she readily understood why Adam had been so anxious to end his New York trip, and she told him so.

The smile Adam gave her was like no other he had bestowed upon her. There was no challenging glint in his deep blue eyes, no sexual invitation. "I wondered if you would appreciate it. I thought you might since you use so much wildlife in your work." He gave her shoulder a squeeze, but somehow his touch was different this time. Companionable was the only word she could think of to describe it. The electricity that usually crackled between them was gone—at least for a moment—and they shared an unexpected rapport. "You'll be able to use more than me for a model out here," he teased good-naturedly.

They arrived at the front of the house, and Adam bounded out, pulling her with him before she could comment on his remark. The front door opened, and a tall middle-aged woman greeted them with a friendly smile. "Adam, it's good to see you. You're just in time, dinner's almost ready."

Before Lysandra could venture a guess at the woman's identity, she was being introduced to Betty Hilder. "Betty manages to keep this big place from becoming a complete shambles," Adam explained. "She also cooks fairly well," he drawled with a teasing glint in his blue eyes that brought an answering gleam to Betty's.

"If you can find anyone else who would put up with you two, she's welcome to the job," she responded tartly. "You don't seem to be suffering none with what I put in front of you."

"Ah, sweet Elizabeth, if you only knew how my boyish heart broke when you ran off with that miserable old man, Dan Hilder. I doubt he appreciates what a jewel he stole away from me. Surely his lowly palate doesn't do justice to your fried chicken?" Adam had struck a dramatic pose during his discourse, feigning a seriousness that was denied by the suppressed curve at the corner of his mouth.

Betty Hilder raised a disdainful brow and put her arm around Lysandra's waist, drawing her into the foyer of the spacious house. "I don't know how well you know our Adam, Lysandra, but if you haven't figured it out already, I advise you not to believe anything he says." Lysandra couldn't resist chuckling with Betty at Adam's affronted expression. "Come on, you've had a long trip. I'll show you to your room. That young fool can bring your bags." She started to lead Lysandra down the corridor when Adam's deep voice interrupted them.

"Put her in Sharon's old room, Betty. She'll be using the studio."

"Are you an artist?" was Betty's quick question, but Lysandra had detected the slight look of surprise on the older woman's face after Adam's instructions. She was forced to answer before she could speculate on Betty's quickly camouflaged expression.

"Yes, I'm a sculptor. That's why I'm here." Her companion's open curiosity prompted Lysandra to explain her presence, even if it did embarrass Adam. In fact, she realized mischievously, after his behavior in the truck, she hoped it would cause him a great deal of embarrassment.

"Adam has agreed to pose for me in exchange for my doing a bronze horse for his father's birthday."

Betty's initial surprise was quickly replaced by a look of comprehension. With an exaggerated wide-eyed gasp, she glanced over her shoulder toward Adam and exclaimed, "In the *nude?*" Receiving confirmation from Lysandra's expression before Adam could deny anything, Betty giggled. "Great! I hope it's not a closed set!"

They both broke into conspiratorial laughter when Adam exploded, "It sure as hell will be!" He shoul-

dered his way past them, carrying Lysandra's bags
and preceded them into the room designated for her
use. A scowl darkened his handsome face as he
muttered something about never living it down if
word reached the ears of the ranch hands and then
stormed back out of the room, leaving the two
women alone with their hilarity.

"Wow!" Betty dabbed at the tears of laughter that
streamed out of her snapping gray eyes with a corner
of her apron. "It's not often anyone manages to get
that boy in such a spot. Done him good, I 'spect."
Bustling about the room, Betty asked, "Are you
really the sculptor who did that bronze horse Clayton
was so fond of? Why, you can't imagine how upset
that man was when it was stolen. He took it almost as
hard as when his favorite horse died." Betty finished
opening the drapes then swiped at an imagined
speck of dust on the glistening surface of the dresser.

The large bedroom had three walls of softly tinted
ivory plaster with the outside wall made of stone and
log like the exterior of the house. A large four-poster
bed stood against one wall, and a big oval, braided
rug lay on the floor by its side. Matching antique
dresser, chest of drawers and tall armoire joined the
chintz-upholstered chaise that completed the furnishings. There were two doors in one of the plastered
walls, one leading to a bathroom and the other into
the studio.

Betty led her into the large well-lit studio, explaining that Adam's younger sister was an artist and that
Clayton had had the room built on for her when

Sharon was in her teens. Sharon had married a few years ago, and the room was no longer used.

Stepping into the studio, Lysandra couldn't imagine a more perfect place to work. A skylight, not unlike the one in her Manhattan apartment, let in the sun and the walls were made almost entirely of glass, providing a view of the grassy meadow and the mountains beyond as well as more light. A long counter with a sink and many cupboards were the only furnishings in the room except for two stools and a large easel that supported an empty canvas.

Explaining that she had some finishing touches to add to their dinner, Betty excused herself and went back to the kitchen. The evening meal would be served in a half hour, giving Lysandra little time to freshen up from the trip.

Moving back to the bedroom, Lysandra unpacked one of her bags, slipped out of her clothing and headed for a quick shower. The warm water gently massaged away some of the tension she was feeling and revived her resolve that, no matter what Adam might be imagining, she fully intended to do nothing more than fulfill the requirements of their business agreement. She would re-create the horse, do her best to portray Adam as *Man of Glory* and maybe even do some sketches of the abundant wildlife to be seen in the mountains that lay just beyond the plateau.

Toweling herself dry, she wrapped her robe around her slight body and went back to the bedroom to dress. Unpacking more of her clothes and hanging them in the beautiful old walnut armoire, she pondered for several minutes over what to wear to dinner. Sensing that the evening would be informal, she chose a cream-colored cotton knit sweater with raglan sleeves and a pair of matching linen slacks.

Running a comb through her long, straight hair and securing it away from her face with tortoise combs, she eyed her reflection in the mirror above the dresser. She refused to think that she might have chosen the softly feminine ensemble because Adam might like it. She wasn't here to gain the interest of the man! That she had applied a touch of cologne to her wrists, temples and the shadowed cleavage between her breasts was only because she enjoyed the scent—a luxury she had indulged in as soon as she was able to afford it. The application of mascara to her already long lashes and a little gloss to highlight her full lips was only to make a good impression on Clayton Honour . . . wasn't it?

6

~~~~~~~~~~~~~~~~

$\mathbf{A}$ short while later Lysandra stepped out of her room and immediately walked smack into a broad male chest. Familiar arms went around her and pulled her even closer. "Umm," Adam said, breathing into her hair. "You smell as good as you feel."

Pushing at his chest, Lysandra fought against his intoxicating nearness, the clean fresh scent of his recently showered body. Her struggles only succeeded in bringing her up against his hard, unyielding length. Her breasts were crushed against him, and she felt her nipples harden, her body instinctively aroused by his touch no matter how hard her conscious mind determined against it. Tipping her head back, she arched away, exposing the graceful line of her throat and unwittingly drawing his knowing gaze to the twin points thrusting beneath her sweater.

"Do that some more, and I'll remember only that you came here to get me alone without any clothes on," he drawled audaciously.

Anger overpowered any other reaction, and she shoved against his chest. "Let me go this instant or I'll forget the whole arrangement!"

He reluctantly released her. "Okay, little lady, but you drive a hard bargain. Let's go to dinner."

Lysandra stumbled away from him and spun on her heel, starting quickly back up the hallway in the general direction of where the dining room was located. She had intended to put several feet between them, but Adam's long stride brought him all too quickly to her side. Her elbow was grasped in his strong hand, and when she tried to pull away he explained with an infuriating smile, "My father sent me to escort you, and I'm not going to disappoint him. He's tried for years to teach me to be a gentleman."

Having no choice, Lysandra resigned herself to Adam's caressing touch and the agony of having to ignore the effect his nearness had upon her as they made their way down the hallway.

Arriving in the large sitting room, she gave a murmur of pleasure at the beautiful paintings and native wall hangings that adorned the rustic interior of the room. The furnishings were an artistic blend of elegance and comfort.

Beautifully cared for antiques of rich mahogany were carefully interspersed with heavier pieces that added a western flavor and informality. It was a perfect marriage of formal elegance and casual utility, highlighted beautifully by the bright Indian weavings and muted oils.

Clayton rose gallantly from a leather wing-back chair near the massive stone fireplace at one end of the large room. "Would you care for a glass of wine or a drink before dinner, my dear?"

"White wine would be fine, thank you," Lysandra murmured and broke away from Adam's hold. Accepting the glass from Clayton, she ignored Adam and walked to one of the oil paintings that flanked the fireplace, standing in silent awe as she recognized the artist. There was no doubt in her mind that it was an original Remington as her eyes scanned the painting, admiring the power of the racing stallions, the determined and fierce expressions on the faces of the proud Indians who rode them. Only Remington could have portrayed the Old West so dramatically, and only an original could exude the depth of color he had used in his work.

The more she saw of Adam's home, the more she was coming to realize just how wealthy a man he was. She must have been crazy to ask him to be her model; she couldn't believe that he had actually agreed. If he could afford an original Remington, why was he so adamant about her being the one to sculpt a horse for his father? As far as she was concerned, there was no comparison between her work and that of a master. It was almost impossible to ignore the feeling that Adam's motives had nothing to do with her talent as an artist, but everything to do with getting her into his bed. Since arriving at the Bar H, he couldn't have been more obvious about his intentions, and she greatly feared that he would eventually succeed if she dropped her guard for more than a second. That fear was reinforced when she sensed she was being watched and turned around to find Adam studying her figure, his electric blue eyes shocking her with their hungry look.

She was grateful when Clayton took her arm to escort her to dinner in the elegant dining room. As Adam took his place at the foot of the table, his attention was diverted away from her, and she used the opportunity to study him. His dark blue knit shirt and lightweight pants didn't brand him a millionaire, but his head was framed by another exquisite painting that hung on the paneled wall behind his chair, and Lysandra was very much aware that the Honours enjoyed a wealth far beyond her comprehension. The wisest thing for her to do would be to pack her bags and take the first plane back to New York.

During dinner the subjects discussed were diverse, from comments on recent political events to a debate over the merits of introducing some new strain of cattle Lysandra thought sounded like "beef-eaters." It was Clayton who seemed most interested in introducing the breed with Adam conservatively emphasizing the traditions of the blooded Herefords they had bred for more than a generation. Lysandra had little to add to the conversation as the two men debated, finally settling down to Adam quizzing his father on various aspects of the ranch that he wanted to catch up on after his absence. She gained the impression that Clayton, while still in his early sixties and enjoying good health, had given over the working reins of the ranch to his son. She learned that Betty's husband, Dan, was the ranch foreman and that she had been their housekeeper for almost twenty years. As the talk became focused on the financial business Adam had been involved with during his trip to New York, Lysandra concentrated on her dinner, feeling more and more out of place until Clayton finally called for coffee to end the meal.

"These two must be boring the socks off you," Betty stated as she brought in the tray and poured steaming cups of coffee. "I could hear them arguing over those new mongrel cows all the way to the kitchen. Seems to me they're so used to dining with only each other, they forget that some folks just don't care about where a good steak comes from so long as it's good and tender." She gave each of the two men a glare that expressed a silent scolding for what Betty clearly thought was rudeness.

Seeing Clayton's embarrassed look, Lysandra quickly denied Betty's condemnation. "Everything was lovely, Betty—even the company." She wasn't actually lying, she had enjoyed at least parts of the discussion. "Thank you for such a delicious meal."

"No trouble." Betty smiled brightly and wiped her hands on her apron. "I'll clear up these dishes and then I'm off."

Clayton suggested they finish their coffee and dessert in the sitting room, apologizing to Lysandra for getting sidetracked with business during the meal and prompting her to talk about herself as they took their places in the next room, she and Clayton upon the long overstuffed couch and Adam in a nearby leather chair. The next two hours passed quickly, and Lysandra was somewhat surprised when Clayton commented on the lateness of the hour and excused himself to go to bed. Being left alone with Adam, Lysandra was about to declare that she was tired as well when Adam prevented her from leaving by getting up from his chair and joining her on the couch.

"Not yet, Lys. Let's stay up a bit longer."

She searched for something to say, all the while aware of the increased sexual tension gathering like a storm between them. Adam was the first to speak, obviously not suffering from the same degree of agitation that was descending on her.

"What do you think of the Bar H?" he asked, shifting his long legs and lifting his booted feet to the top of the coffee table. "And my father?"

"I think you're a very lucky man in both respects." Now was as good a time as any to lay her cards on the table, and Lysandra wanted everything out in the open. "But you've made it clear that by coming here, I've signed up for more than I bargained for, and I can't have that."

"You know what they say about striking bargains with the devil." Twinkling blue eyes were far too close as Lysandra swung her head around to face him.

On a noticeable intake of breath, she blurted, "And exactly what's that supposed to mean?"

His quick grin was swiftly covered as he reached for his coffee cup and emptied it. "I'm finding it very hard not to tease you, Lys. I don't think you've had much practice in the fine old art of bantering. You rise to the bait so quickly. Didn't you have any brothers?"

"No," she said hesitantly, refusing to give in to the odd urge she suddenly had to divulge something of her early life to him. She took a deep breath and attempted to divert him back to the matter at hand. "I don't like the way you've been acting since we got here. I don't want everyone to think that we're . . . that you're . . ."

"How have I been acting?" he asked, knowing full well that she didn't want to explain.

When she didn't immediately answer, he edged closer, pressing his thigh against her leg, picking up a strand of her silky hair and running it through his fingers. "I don't know any other way to behave with a beautiful woman than to show her that I find her desirable. What's so wrong with that?"

The nerve of him—acting so innocent! As if he didn't have the slightest idea what was bothering her. She wanted to tell him what she thought was wrong with his behavior but couldn't seem to remember a word of the several speeches she had imagined herself giving him on the subject. He thought she was beautiful . . . desirable . . . "Adam, I don't want you to think that . . ."

"I don't want you to think either." Adam placed a hand under her chin and lifted her lips to his waiting mouth.

Already addicted to his intoxicating taste, Lysandra didn't stand a chance as he satisfied her need with an expert thoroughness that stopped rational thought—exactly as he had wished. She endured only one brief second of alarming dismay before his demanding tongue enticed her to his will, and she yielded to the heavenly seduction of his mouth.

His thumb gently stroked the corner of her lips and the tender gesture made the breath catch in her throat. As he held her, she felt as if he thought of her as some delicate bud he must awaken carefully. She made no protest when his other hand slid beneath her sweater and meandered across her bare skin. It felt good, very good, and she didn't have the power to deny what she had craved from the first time he had taken her into his arms.

"Touch me, Lys," he whispered, drawing one of her hands to his chest, making her feel the steadily increasing beat of his heart. "Learn my body as I want to learn yours."

He made it easier for her, pulling his shirt out from the waistband of his pants as he placed her hand beneath the material and held her palm against the smooth skin of his side.

As an artist, she had wanted to feel each strong line of muscle he possessed, but it was the woman in her who touched him now, the woman who needed to know everything about him. When he groaned in the back of his throat and pulled the shirt off over his head, she hesitated only a second before using both hands to reach out and touch the gleaming, golden shoulders that were at last revealed to her devouring eyes. Her fingers trembled, tracing the softly curling hair that spread across the massive chest she had known would be as well-developed as the naked Adonis whom she had conceived of but never thought to find.

"Oh, Adam." She could hardly speak but the impassioned tone was enough for him to realize how she felt, and he deftly lifted her across his lap and in one swift movement had pulled her sweater over her head. One large hand pressed her head to his shoulder while he used the other to unclasp her bra and slide it off. Breathing in his spicy scent, her cheek rubbing heatedly over the warm burnished skin, she gasped against his chest as he cupped one breast in his palm and used each finger to entice the soft mound to a stiffened peak.

His fingers threaded into her dark hair, sending the tortoise combs sliding to the floor and directing her face back to his so that he could ignite their mouths with the same fire that burned in her breast. The low groans of pleasure he emitted excited her to the point of madness as her fingers encircled his male nipples and painted tormenting patterns across the hair-roughened skin that surrounded them, then fell to her sides as he arched his back and pushed her down upon the soft cushions.

His eyes were purple flames as he leaned over her, moving his body to lie over hers on the wide couch, entangling his long legs with hers so that she could feel the aggressive strength in them.

"I've wanted you like this from the first moment I saw you," he rasped thickly, the purple flames growing darker as his eyes consumed the quivering feminine curves displayed so provocatively before him. "You're so small . . . but the perfect fit for me," he murmured, then showed her what he meant by letting her feel the full force of his desire. His weight descended against her, legs, hips, chest, as he placed one hand on each side of her face and his lips came down on her mouth with a raw and forceful hunger she hadn't felt in him before. It was then that the full import of what she was doing was brought home to her, when the undeniable hardness of him pressed between her legs and her naked breasts were flattened beneath the weight of his all-male brawn.

Even then it might not have been enough to restore her senses if she had been able to breathe, but she couldn't; she felt smothered and began to struggle in earnest. Using her hands to push against him, it took several seconds before he realized she was fighting him. "You're right." He shifted his body so she could get her breath and lifted himself off the couch, then gathered her in his arms. "This isn't the right place to make love to you. It's certainly not my intention to smother you."

She would have ended it then and there, but he didn't give her the chance, bending his head to her mouth and damming the protesting words she had planned to utter. His long legs took them down the hall to her bedroom and before she was allowed to say another word, he had laid her down upon the four-poster bed and had come down beside her.

"Adam, stop," she managed to choke out while his lips and hands adored her throbbing nipples. "Please, you have to listen to me."

Trembling fingers clutched the blond hair of his head, felt the throbbing pulse at his temples before he lifted his face away from her breasts. "I am listening to you, Lys." He cupped both hands beneath the burgeoning curves his lips had just left. "Listening to your body cry out for mine, feeling your racing heartbeat beg for my touch."

"No!" she cried out and twisted away from him, grabbing the edge of the coverlet and pulling it up over her bosom. "I'm not another of the women you've brought out here to satisfy your needs. I don't go to bed with a man who wants nothing more from me than séx. I'm not like that."

The purple heat died in his eyes and was replaced by a glacial blue. "What the hell are you talking about?"

"Can you deny that I'm the most recent of a long line of women who've been brought here to share your bed?"

"Who told you that?"

She saw no denial in his cold gaze and knew she was doing the right thing. "No one had to tell me. I could see it in their faces. Betty, your father—they both think I came because I'm your latest lover, and you've hardly tried to set them straight." Her eyes were deep pools of accusation.

"That's because I fully intend for that to happen."

Adam sat up, swinging his legs to rest over the side of the bed as he took a deep breath. "If you're honest, you'll admit you want it, too—wanted it tonight."

"I'll admit I wanted you, but I don't want a casual affair with you. For me, sex means commitment, and you aren't offering that, are you?"

"Commitment!" His mouth twisted, and he came off the bed in a violent surge of motion. "You wanted my body, sweetheart. Your eyes are always undressing me, your breasts tighten whenever I get near you, your voice gets low with passion. You weren't after commitment until you saw this place and realized the money it must take to keep it going."

"That's a rotten lie!" Lysandra retorted, tears shimmering in her eyes as she digested the contempt in his voice. "Get out! Get out of here!"

"I'm going, but this isn't the end." Adam grabbed the coverlet and pulled it away from her, his eyes insolently raking over her before he dropped it, swung on his heel and strode toward the door. "Eventually, you'll hurt as bad as I'm hurting and when that time comes, commitment will have nothing to do with the decision you make to come to me. Maybe you're not the type to lust after money, but I've got all the proof I need that you lust after me, and one of these days you'll admit it."

He didn't slam the door behind him as he left, but the cold metallic click it made as he closed it demonstrated his anger. The finality of the sound repeated itself over and over again inside her head as the night hours slowly slipped away.

7

Lysandra sipped her breakfast coffee and returned the smile Clayton Honour beamed at her from across the table. "You make a good breakfast, Mr. Honour," she complimented, hoping he wouldn't comment on the telltale shadows beneath her eyes or the fact that she had eaten a very small portion of the mammoth breakfast he had prepared.

"Thank you, Lys, but please call me Clayton. I'm glad you enjoyed it. I didn't want you to think that everyone had abandoned you on your first morning. Work begins as soon as the sun rises around here, and Betty serves a mile-high stack of hotcakes over at their place around six."

Instantly aware that his remarks might have made Lysandra feel guilty, he reached across the table and patted her shoulder. "But there's no need for you to get up so early. It's barely eight now. Even I don't get up and at 'em as early as I used to. It's one of my privileges to enjoy a leisurely breakfast at a later hour. I'm glad I had someone to share it with today.''

Lysandra was surprised that she had slept at all and more surprised that she had still managed to wake up as punctually as she had originally planned. She had wanted to get out of bed early, unpack her supplies and equipment, then start work, taking advantage of the clear morning light. Last night, she had lain awake for what seemed like hours remembering the feel of Adam's lips on hers, his long hard body weighing heavily against her smaller, softer curves. His large hands running lightly over her body had aroused her to such a pitch that as she lay alone later and recalled every moment of their sensual interlude, she admitted that her refusal to allow him to spend the night making love to her had been as much a denial of her own desires as his. She had never had so much difficulty stilling wandering hands and pulling away from heated embraces with other men. Why Adam?

She forced herself to concentrate on Clayton's description of the people who worked and lived on the ranch. It sounded almost like a departmentalized corporation as he outlined each facet of the work being done on the huge Honour holdings. She was amazed at the technology involved in running a modern-day ranch and was especially fascinated by Clayton's discussion of the computerized feeding of some of the stock.

"Adam would have more than enough to keep

him busy if he concentrated on the other divisions of the Honour Corporation, but I guess being a fourth-generation rancher, it's in his blood to keep a working hand on the reins."

"What do you mean? Is there more involved than just the ranch?" was Lysandra's startled inquiry.

Clayton's blue eyes glittered with amusement before he answered, "Well, I'm sure Adam mainly thinks of himself as a rancher, but he has a few other responsibilities as well. I guess he didn't explain much about the family company, did he?"

Lysandra fought the heated blush that rose in her cheeks as she recalled that Adam's discussions had usually been centered on his plans to share her bed. "No . . . he talked about owning a ranch, nothing else."

"Well, let me give you a little background, Lys." Clayton seemed more than happy to elaborate and, unlike his son, eager to provide her with the family's history.

"A century ago, my grandpa came out here and acquired a little land, ran a few cows and even managed to find a little silver in the mountains. Instead of drinking his profits away like most, he kept buying up more land along with some of the claims of prospectors who thought their silver and gold had fizzled out. He married one of the pretty school-teachers they used to import from back East.

"You know, there were so few women out here, that the men hardly had the patience to wait for enough children to warrant a school before they started advertising for teachers. The teachers had to submit a picture with their applications." Clayton winked across the table. "It was really more a mail-order bride proposition than any desire to educate the few children in the area. Most of those young gals only lasted a few months teaching school."

Lysandra giggled as she imagined a long lineup of lonely men ogling the new "schoolmarm" as soon as the woman had arrived.

"Anyway, by the time my pa came along and managed to grow up, the ranch was showing a pretty good profit running cattle. Not satisfied with that, Pa started breeding horses and investigating the possibilities of working the old mines, thinking that with better methods he might extract the remaining ore. He managed to pick out just enough to keep his interest going in the mines.

"He sent me off to college and made me study geology. Finally, Pa's interest in mining paid off. We discovered minerals the early miners didn't know anything about—molybdenum mainly, as well as a little oil on some of our other holdings. Now we dabble in just about every industry Colorado has to offer except the tourist trade." Clayton paused to take a long sip of his coffee.

Lysandra wondered what molybdenum was, but Clayton wasn't finished with his story.

"You know, women are still pretty scarce out here on the western slope, and both my pa and myself had to import our brides from the East. Like Grandpa, Pa married a schoolteacher, but I guess I was a bit more sophisticated." Clayton paused a moment and gazed out of the window toward the mountains. His smile disappeared and was replaced by a distant look, as if his eyes weren't focusing on the scenery but on painful events from the past.

Lysandra waited quietly, sensing that what Clayton might choose to disclose would be far more personal than his previous narrative. Her hand instinctively moved toward him, wanting to erase whatever pain the memory of his wife was causing him. Her small palm rested lightly on his large, gnarled hand.

For several moments, only the sounds of a squawking jay and the chattering of a small squirrel busily running back and forth between the ground and a tall aspen broke the quiet.

"Marian was the prettiest girl I ever did see, and I couldn't believe how lucky I was when she agreed to marry me. We had some wonderful years together before the loneliness of this life got to her, and she went back East. She needed lots of people around her; she was used to a constant social whirl, but that's not how it is up here in the mountains. If we'd moved over to Denver, maybe things would have been different, but I couldn't leave this valley for the city and she just . . ." His voice dropped lower, grew softer as he described the woman he had loved, prompting Lysandra to tighten her clasp on his hand.

"Mr. . . . Clayton . . ." She wanted to offer some sort of comfort but couldn't find the words to help erase the loneliness she could discern on his lined face. Reading the compassion in her eyes, his lips spread in a sheepish smile, a smile so much like his son's but without Adam's cynical twist.

The screen door opened with a loud bang. "Well, I see you two are getting along very well," Adam announced coldly, his stony gaze resting pointedly on Lysandra's and Clayton's clasped hands.

Startled by his censorious tone, Lysandra jumped up and clumsily jerked her hand away beneath the table. The tall figure who stood by the door, legs firmly planted apart, back rigid, had gotten her full attention if that had been his intent. The morning sun streamed through the screen behind him and highlighted his golden hair, glistening across the flesh of his corded forearms where he had rolled up the cuffs of his work shirt. Faded denim jeans were slung low on his slim hips, outlining his lean muscular legs and undoubted virility. It was only the accusation he had made to her the night before about her eyes continually divesting him of his clothing that kept her from doing it yet again.

Hiding her interest behind the large mug of coffee she held with both hands, she surreptitiously watched him remove his well-worn Stetson, then peel the short gloves from his hands. She heard the slap of leather as he straightened the gloves against his thigh before tossing them onto the counter. As he walked to the stainless steel sink, she stared wide-eyed as he lowered his blond head beneath the faucet, then grabbed a towel and quickly wiped the water from his face and neck. He washed his hands with quick, efficient movements, then dried them off with the towel, walked to the stove, tested the coffeepot to make sure it was still hot before reaching for one of the mugs hanging on the wall.

When he turned back to them, Lysandra managed to keep her expression bland, relieved that Clayton was the one who had the courage to address Adam's undiminished scowl.

"You're right," Clayton remarked casually on Adam's initial greeting. "Lysandra has been gracious enough to act interested as I bored her with our family history. I'm sure she'll enjoy your company far more than that of an old codger like me."

"I wasn't bored, Clayton," Lysandra assured him, glaring at Adam from beneath the sweep of her long lashes. "And you're hardly an 'old codger.'" Clayton had fast become her friend, and the smile she bestowed on him was warmly affectionate. Her comment brought an easy grin to Clayton's face, but Adam's scowl didn't alter. Lysandra was confused by his dark mood. Was Adam displeased that she and his father enjoyed each other's company? Or was he still angry about last night?

A steaming mug of coffee in hand, Adam slid his big frame down beside her on the oak bench, forcing her to slide over. "I'm surprised you're even up," he jabbed mockingly. "I thought all you city girls slept your mornings away. You did sleep well in that big four-poster, didn't you? I've always found it quite comfortable." His suggestive words couldn't be misinterpreted, and Lysandra's cheeks flamed as she gave a swift glance at his father to see if he had given Adam's remark the same interpretation she had. If there had been any doubt as to what Adam was implying, it was erased when he slid his arm around her waist and drew her tightly to his side.

Her embarrassment grew, but Clayton seemed unaffected by Adam's actions. There was no escape from the position she was in. The wall of the built-in eating space hemmed her in on one side, and Adam's unyielding body formed a formidable fortress on the other. Both men ignored her presence while Adam explained to his father what he had been doing so far that morning and what work was being undertaken for the day. The only indication Lysandra had that Adam was aware of her sitting beside him was the tightening of his arm around her every time she tried to put a few inches of space between them.

The warmth of his body burned against her, and she could detect the scent of the fresh outdoors emanating from his clothes. His hair smelled like the wind, and she held her breath to prevent herself from responding to it, unable to quell the painful lurch in her chest that occurred whenever he came near.

Her denim-clad thigh was pressed tightly against his, and she restlessly slanted her legs away from him, but the escape from his touch was short-lived as he nonchalantly moved his thigh back into searing contact with hers. He was branding her as his in front of his father as surely as if he had heated an iron and placed it against her skin. Why? What compelled him to establish her as his property? That he might be jealous of the companionable time she had spent over breakfast with Clayton seemed too ridiculous to contemplate.

Not being able to withstand Adam's behavior nor his possessive actions toward her for another second, Lysandra broke into the conversation and asked to be excused so that she could get started unpacking her crates of supplies. Clayton readily accepted her excuse, but her relief was brief as Adam volunteered to accompany her. She was forced to wait by his side as he finished his conversation with his father. Though he had slid off the bench to allow her to leave it, he had immediately returned his arm to her waist when she rose and once again held her imprisoned tightly at his side. His granite hold didn't loosen until they left the kitchen.

Steaming anger threatened to erupt inside her as she walked briskly ahead of him to the studio. She could sense the tension in his big body as he followed closely behind, but she was so caught up in her own anger her only objective was to get out of Clayton's earshot and tell Adam exactly what she thought of his behavior.

As soon as they had stepped into the studio and closed the door behind them, Lysandra whirled around. "Just what were you trying to prove? How dare you treat me like some sort of possession when I thought I had made it perfectly clear to you last night what our relationship was going to be!"

"You know perfectly well what our relationship is going to be! You're just taking your sweet time recognizing it." He stood belligerently before her, his long, muscled legs planted slightly apart and his powerful arms folded across his chest. His penetrating gaze riveted on her blazing eyes, eyes that could be so soft and warm, warm enough to melt any man. Despite his anger with her, he felt his body tighten in reaction to her. That same tiny figure who stood before him, taut with fury, could mold so softly against him. He took a step toward her, but she backed away and around the table standing in the middle of the room.

"It's *you* who won't recognize what our relationship is! You acted like a jealous lover in front of your father." She went on, taking courage from the man-made barrier she had placed between them. "How could you imply that we had shared a bed last night?"

"Should I be jealous?" he countered angrily. "For a few seconds, we did share that bed."

Ignoring the last statement, she attacked. "You have no right to be jealous—you have to care about someone to be jealous of them, and you don't care anything about me. . . . I'm just some kind of challenge to you because I haven't immediately hopped into your bed!"

Adam advanced into the room and stopped before the table, unfolding his arms and leaning menacingly forward as his large hands gripped the edge. "Don't ever let me catch you making a play for my dad." His words came out slowly, deadly. "Is that understood?"

Her heated anger fell away and was replaced by a cold horror. "Make a play for your father! What kind of woman do you think I am?" Before he started to answer she held up her hand, shaking her head with renewed fury. "No, don't answer. I can guess what kind of woman you think I am. You've made that perfectly clear."

She and Clayton had enjoyed a lovely breakfast together, and Adam had walked in on a rare moment of shared understanding between friends. How could he possibly misconstrue it as something else? Her happiness was shattered. Adam's angry interpretation was the greatest insult she had ever received.

The light streaming in the skylight overhead fell on his hair, making it glow with almost a halo effect, but the man was hardly a suitable candidate for a halo! He was without any doubt the most infuriating man she had ever met. She felt as if she had been caught up in a whirlwind since their first meeting—a mass of conflicting emotions had erupted within her and threatened every part of the very safe world she had painstakingly created for herself.

They stood glaring at each other across the table, each daring the other to look away and admit defeat. Not breaking the gaze, but lowering her voice, Lysandra tersely announced, "I don't think we need unpack my supplies. I think it would be best if we canceled our agreement and I went back to New York."

As soon as she made the announcement, she turned away and slowly walked toward the back of the room, gazing miserably out at the jagged peaks that could be seen in the distance. Those mountains had seemed so beautiful to her yesterday, but today they appeared oppressive and threatening. They, like the man behind her, were much too powerful, too overwhelming.

Man of Glory might never be finished as she would like, but somehow that no longer seemed as important to her. She could go back to New York, sketch Adam from memory and possibly complete the work, but it wouldn't be the same without him. Without a doubt, she would have trouble depicting the vital essence of the man, his strength and beauty without having him as the life model during the creative process, but he was making it impossible for her to stay.

She must stoically resign herself to do the best she could under the changed circumstances. There was still plenty of time before she had to send the piece to the foundry in order for it to be cast into bronze, still enough time to do the final finishing before the Bernard-Wilcox show if, during the time remaining, she concentrated fully on her craft.

There was no way she could go on with things as they were, having to continually contend with the tormenting distraction of Adam's addictive lovemaking. It felt too good to be in his arms, and she knew she wouldn't be able to fend him off much longer. Where could an affair with him possibly lead? Nowhere! He might forget the short summer interlude as soon as she left, but could she forget him? Would she find it possible to put the whole affair behind her as she was certain he'd easily be able to do?

Carried away by the disturbing flow of her thoughts, she didn't notice that he had taken a position nearby and could see the distress written clearly across her face. The slender curves that had entranced him to the point where he had practically carried her off on his shoulder like some lovelorn caveman suddenly seemed too fragile to carry the burdens expressed in her dark eyes.

He recognized that kind of pain, and the need to protect her claimed him, erasing every shred of anger from his face. When he moved up behind her, all he wanted was to shelter her from the inner agony she was suffering. His hands descending upon her shoulders made her jump, and she tried to pull away.

"Don't, Lys." His voice was unbelievably soft, a disturbed heaviness in the warm breath that grazed her cheek. He ran his fingers lightly over her shoulders and down her arms, then locked his hands together at her waist and gently pulled her back against his chest. She tried to remain rigid, expecting him to begin making more of the demands she found so difficult to withstand, but instead he stood without speaking, simply holding her in the secure circle of his arms. Unable to go on fighting, she slumped back and closed her eyes.

Keeping her enclosed in the tender stronghold of his embrace, he placed a soft kiss on the top of her hair. "I was wrong, Lys. I'll admit it." She could feel the suppressed tension in his body, sense the effort he was making to soothe away her anxiety at being held so closely against him. "I know I haven't been truthful with you, but I've wanted you so badly from that first meeting in New York that I didn't stop to consider anything else. I still want you, but I realize you need more time. That night in your studio, I would have done anything to insure you'd end up in my bed. I couldn't stay in New York any longer, so I agreed to pose for you if you'd come to Colorado with me."

Hearing him admit that getting her into his bed had been his plan from the very beginning, Lysandra stiffened in his arms. She had known it all along, but having him confirm it made it impossible for her to continue rationalizing away the feelings she had experienced the night they'd met. Needing him as a model had provided her with a logical excuse to explore the new and wonderful sensations he had awakened within her. It was true that he hadn't exactly been honest with her, but she hadn't been honest either—especially with herself.

She pulled away, but he wouldn't let her go. "Adam . . . I . . ."

"Shh, don't talk, just listen. Hear me out. There's something unique happening between us, and you know it as well as I do. I apologize for bringing you out here under false pretenses, it was a pretty underhanded ploy, but I really needed to get back here, and I sure as hell didn't want to leave you behind. There's something about you that keeps pulling at me. It started at the Parkers' party when I turned around and saw you walking toward me. I didn't want to take the chance of never seeing you again without exploring it further. Won't you admit that you feel it, too?" His voice was a baritone rumble, and Lysandra fought the need to turn in his arms and give herself up to the sensual plea.

"Maybe there is, Adam," she whispered finally. "But I can't fall into bed with you just because you want me, and there's this sexual chemistry building between us."

"Why not? I know there's a lot of emotion hidden behind that cool reserve you show the world. No one who created that bronze horse you won't part with could be without passion. The woman I held in my arms last night was burning up with need. Why can't you admit it? Why do you erect such self-destructive barriers?"

He rested his chin on the top of her head, his breath a caress gently moving the silken strands of her hair. She could feel the steady beat of his heart against her back and the comforting warmth and strength of his body against hers. "You don't understand. You . . ."

"Has someone hurt you, Lys? Another man?"

How could she explain that so many people had hurt her while she was growing up that she'd eventually lost count? No. It wasn't any heartless lover from her past who had disappointed her. Her fear of emotional involvement stemmed from the lack of any such fulfilling emotion. The nomadic life she had led had precluded establishing any emotional ties. She had quickly learned that it was safer not to feel any affection for her foster parents because they were quickly replaced by new ones. Not one of the families who had made a place for her in their homes had been willing to make a place for her in their hearts, or had been willing to commit themselves to her and provide a permanent home for the lonely,

withdrawn little girl with the skinny body and enor-
mous eyes. And she had found it was far safer not to
commit herself to any of them. Instead she gave her
affections freely to the animals she sketched and only
dreamed about the family who might one day accept
her as their own, the kind of loving parent Adam had
enjoyed his entire life.

"There wasn't another man." She loosened
Adam's grip at her waist and stepped away. After a
long tension-filled silence, she cried, "This isn't
working, Adam. I'm going back to New York."

Inwardly trembling, she watched the change come
over him. His fingers curled into fists that clenched
tightly at his sides, and when he spoke his voice was
determinedly flat. "No. You're not walking out on
this. I agreed to pose for you, and I honor my
commitments. I may have dragged you out here for
another reason, but I gave you my word, and out
here a man's word still means something."

"We can't work together," she insisted, but
couldn't sustain his piercing regard or face the smol-
dering anger that detonated within him.

"I said I'll do it, and you'll damn well stay here
until you've got what you came for." He turned his
back on her but she could see the coiled rage that
stiffened his spine.

"We'll keep our relationship nice and safe, *little
girl.* I won't lay a hand on you." He took a few angry
steps toward the door, then stopped and turned back
to face her once more. "Get unpacked and set up. I'll
be back here tomorrow morning. I can spare you

one hour every morning between eight and nine. Will that be enough?"

The inflection in his voice implied that it had better be enough, for it was all the time she was going to get. Unable to find her voice, she gave him a short affirmative nod, hurt by the cutting edge in his tone when he had labeled her a child, unaware that the reason for his anger was because he couldn't reach the defensive little girl who either couldn't or wouldn't tell him of her past.

8

A coolly impersonal Adam reported to the studio the next morning exactly on time. Lysandra hadn't seen him during the remainder of the previous day and so she had busied herself with unpacking. By midafternoon she had arranged her supplies and readied the room to accommodate her work. A single bench stood in the spot she had determined had the best light, and she placed a folding screen nearby.

Last night, Adam hadn't made an appearance at dinner, so she and Clayton had dined alone, neither remarking on Adam's absence. Their conversation had been congenial, but the closeness they had enjoyed that morning hadn't been there. Pleading fatigue, Lysandra had excused herself early and retired to her room where, after a long soak in the bath, she had tried to concentrate on a paperback novel she had brought with her until she eventually had fallen asleep.

"Well?" Adam inquired impatiently.

She indicated the screen in the corner where he could disrobe, then stationed herself on a high stool, sketchbook and charcoal in hand, waiting nervously for Adam to reappear. Schooling herself to maintain a professional attitude, she kept her voice calm and her features noncommittal when he came out, completely nude, from behind the screen. All that had been hinted at beneath the snug-fitting jeans was now revealed, but Lysandra didn't show her stunned reaction at the sight of him, saying nothing as she opened her sketch pad.

Maintain your distance and don't touch him, she lectured herself. You had plenty of experience drawing nude male bodies while you were in school. This is no different, remember that.

"Where do you want me?" he asked calmly, standing directly beneath the skylight, completely without modesty.

She'd placed the wooden bench in the middle of the studio and covered it with a drape of muslin. "Lean against that bench first," she ordered. "I want to see how the light plays across your features."

Without a word he followed her instructions. After a few additional directions, she had his head tilted perfectly to catch the early morning sun and was sketching busily. He stood motionless while she began working, appreciating his ability to maintain a natural pose.

The light played across his golden body, highlighting his beautiful hair to a metallic sheen. His wide shoulders and muscled chest offered the planes and angles she wanted to depict. The corded muscles in his arms and thighs produced the lines and shadows that would lend themselves beautifully to the highly polished bronze sculpture that was evolving more clearly in her artist's mind with each passing moment. He was *Man of Glory,* an ideally proportioned human being.

The haze of curling golden hair that covered so much of his body glowed in the light, glorifying the lines and power of his structure. Her hands shook momentarily, her fingertips remembering the feel of those smooth muscles across his chest, gliding through the curling cloud of hair. She experienced an overwhelming urge to cross the space between them and run her fingers over his entire body, but then hauled herself up short.

Stop it! she commanded inwardly. Remember, life models are not to be touched and ogled. Think of them as a bowl of fruit—a graphic problem of light and depth, planes and angles. Wasn't that the lecture her beginning art class had received during their first session? Concentrate on the lines and curves—not on the whole.

This piece would be the culmination of her years of training. She would depict his beauty by portraying his power, strength and vital force in abstract motion. His body would have been an ideal model for the great masters of the past, even though it was more heavily muscled than many of the works of Michelangelo, and not as massive as some of Rodin's. Adam wouldn't express the innocence of *David,* or the pondering thought of *The Thinker,* but he would depict the elemental simplicity of the human form, the height of perfected creation.

She glanced back to his face and found him squinting, blinking back tears caused by the bright sunlight falling directly into his eyes. "I . . . I'm sorry, Adam," she apologized. "Close your eyes, and in a few more seconds turn your face away from the sun. I'm almost finished with this detail."

Moments later, she repositioned him verbally, guiding his movements until he'd obtained the position she had in mind. She quickly sketched each pose, not completely satisfied with any one of them, but knowing she was getting closer to the image she wanted after each one. She didn't realize how much time had gone by until Adam moved out of position and stretched, announcing bluntly that her time was up. With no additional comment, he went behind the screen, dressed and abruptly left the studio.

All that week, the pattern was repeated. He would dutifully report to her studio in the morning then disappear for the rest of the day. If he did share the dinner hour with Lysandra and Clayton, his manner was polite but strictly impersonal.

For Lysandra, their first session together had been the most difficult, but she couldn't tell how Adam felt about being her model. His face never revealed any emotion other than the natural strain he felt by the end of each sitting.

The sessions were conducted in almost complete silence, except for the few comments Lysandra made as she directed him, and the scratching sound of her rapidly moving charcoal crossing the rough surface of her sketch pad. The time had passed smoothly as Lysandra established a working routine. She remained in the studio until noon, completing her sketches and contemplating her requirements for the next day's session, then she joined Clayton and Betty in the kitchen for lunch.

There had been only one minor lapse in her professional demeanor and that had occurred because Adam's foot had accidentally slipped off the bench. He had muttered a startled oath that had broken her concentration, and when she'd looked up she didn't see the ideal she was mentally creating, but the real man. A throbbing warmth had spread from her stomach, radiating across her breasts and down through her loins as she waited for him to return to the position she had instructed him to take. Her eyes had hungrily followed his movements while she had taken several deep, calming breaths to regain control of herself. At first she'd thought Adam hadn't noticed, but then she spied the slight raising of one brow and the satisfied lift at the corner of his mouth. She'd been grateful when that particular session had come to a close, and she no longer had to fight to maintain her composure.

On the rare evenings that Adam appeared for

dinner, he would generally arrive at the house, go directly to his room, shower, then join them at the table. Immediately after the meal, he would excuse himself and disappear into his study to go over the paperwork involved in running the Honour Corporation.

Her afternoons were spent in the studio refining her sketches and beginning work on the clay form she would use. Whenever she felt overpowered by her intense involvement with *Man of Glory,* she'd start working on the clay model of the horse she'd promised to make for Clayton's birthday. She took advantage of the opportunity she had to observe the horses grazing in the paddocks around the house, and sometimes she left the studio to spend a few pleasant hours playing with the two young colts she had discovered in the stable. The stablehand had explained that they were descendants of Hurricane.

She wasn't aware that her fingers were creating a rendition of the animal that closely resembled the one she had kept for herself, being much too excited about the ease with which she was able to bring the savage form to life. The violent movement she infused within the beast became an outlet for her suppressed emotions, and when she returned her attention to *Man of Glory,* she was capable of giving it her best concentrated effort.

As the days passed, her relationship with Clayton began to blossom once again. Their discussions often centered on art, and Lysandra was impressed by the knowledge Clayton had of the art world and amazed at the collection he so proudly displayed in his home. In addition to the Remington, Clayton had some works by established Colorado artists. A Thompson and an oil by Enrique Montenegro adorned the walls.

Liberally sprinkled amongst these works were watercolors and a few abstract prints done by his daughter, Sharon. Clayton talked glowingly about his daughter and was proud of her accomplishments. Her work centered mainly on the scenery displayed so vividly around the ranch, but the picture Clayton was proudest of was the small oil portrait Sharon had done of her little daughter, Marilee. The child's delightful likeness held a place of honor on one wall of the living room.

Like any proud grandfather, Clayton spoke of his small granddaughter with besotted affection. If the portrait was a good likeness, little Marilee Johnson was a beautiful child. Sharon and her family lived in Denver, and it was obvious that Clayton yearned to see them more often. His daughter apparently enjoyed a very busy life in Denver, and her visits to the Bar H were infrequent. Clayton joked that a range of mountains separated the two halves of the state and unfortunately the family, like the land, was split by the Rockies. Lysandra found herself jealously yearning for the affection Clayton displayed toward his children and grandchild. If only she had had someone like Clayton to love her when she had been growing up, even the formidable mountains wouldn't have kept her from his side.

He didn't bring up the subject of his wife again,

and she wondered if she were still living. How long ago had Marian left this beautiful valley for life in the city? Clayton was a man with so much love to share that Lysandra, who had known so little in her life, couldn't imagine how any woman could throw it away. Recognizing her growing affection for Clayton, she purposely held herself back in an effort to protect herself from the hurt she knew would come when she had to leave.

It wasn't in Clayton to make demands on her. He quietly accepted whatever she was willing to give and gently tried to draw her out during their long evenings together. It was only her own anxiety and Adam's scowl whenever he was around them that kept her from completely letting her guard down in Clayton's company.

The days passed in this routine until she no longer required Adam's presence in the studio; by the second week she was concentrating on applying wax to the clay form to detail the work. One morning Adam surprised both her and Clayton by joining them at breakfast and announcing that she wouldn't be working that day. When she started to protest, he stopped her with, "You've been at it for too long and need some time off. You told me that you learned to ride when you were a teenager. Wouldn't you like to take advantage of the ranch and come on a ride up into the mountains? You can bring your sketch pad if it'll make you feel less guilty. I'll even try to find some interesting animals for you."

This was an entirely different Adam than the one

she was used to. She found herself staring at the crinkled laugh lines beside his sky-blue eyes, and before she could offer any further resistance to his unexpected invitation, Clayton had taken Adam's side, voicing his hearty approval of the plan.

"You've holed up in the house for days and need to get out. Don't worry, I'll clear up these dishes; you run along and get ready. Be sure to take a jacket, it can get mighty cool up in the high country." He pushed her out of the kitchen, telling her that he wouldn't allow her to stay inside the house on such a beautiful day. She wasn't aware of the conspiratorial expressions exchanged by the two men as she followed orders and went to her room.

She had to agree that she needed a break and was excited by the prospect of being on a horse after so many years. She had dressed that morning with the assumption that she'd be working in the studio all day, where the greenhouse effect provided by the large picture windows made it quite warm. Shorts and halters had become her daily uniform while working.

Slipping them off quickly, she pulled on a pair of jeans and a long-sleeved cotton blouse, then rummaged around in the armoire until she came upon her old riding boots. Luckily she had remembered to pack them. They had been included as an after-thought, and now she was glad she'd had the presence of mind that hectic morning to remember she owned them.

Her long ebony hair was already pulled up and

secured in a ponytail to keep it from falling across her face while she worked; now it would serve the same purpose during her ride. She hadn't brought a hat, so she tucked a scarf inside her pocket and grabbed her embroidered denim jacket. She made a quick dash into the studio for her sketch pad, a box of charcoal, her movie camera and film, then went to the kitchen to rejoin Adam and Clayton.

"Now you look like one of us," Clayton complimented her as she walked in. "Except for the camera. Prepared for anything, aren't you?"

"Where work is concerned," Adam interjected, "I've learned that she's very familiar with the tools of her trade."

"Thank you," she said, deciding to take his words at face value. "I always carry a camera in case there's not enough time to sit down and sketch."

"You may be an artist, but you look more like a cowgirl," Adam said. "But there's one thing missing, and every good cowgirl should have one." He lifted a hat from its peg by the kitchen door and placed it on her head. It fit perfectly. His knuckles grazed her skin as he slid the wooden bead beneath her chin to secure the hat. A smile slanted his mouth. It was the first genuine smile she had seen in so many days that Lysandra unconsciously lowered her guard and returned it, basking in his approval.

"It's my sister's hat," he explained. "She keeps a few things here for when she visits." There was a slight touch of wistfulness in his tone that indicated that he missed her.

Lysandra realized with a pang that his smile hadn't been for her, but had been inspired by thoughts of Sharon. He turned away to reach for the saddlebags Clayton was holding, and Lysandra tried to force down the spurt of envy she felt. How lucky he was to have such enjoyable family memories.

The two men had been busy while she had been changing. Sandwiches had been assembled, wrapped and packed into one saddlebag along with a thermos of coffee and a bottle of wine. Adam relieved her of her camera and other supplies, stowing them in the other bag. Without further conversation, he propelled her out of the door and toward the stable.

The excursion hadn't been as spur of the moment as she'd first supposed, but was obviously a well-planned event. Their two horses were already saddled and tied to a post just outside the stable door. A large roan thoroughbred danced impatiently next to the dainty black mare Adam declared was her mount.

She gave him a half-accusing glare. "Exactly when did you start planning this outing?"

A slow, engaging smile spread across his face before he answered. "My father suggested it some time ago," he admitted with such warmth and humor in his voice that Lysandra couldn't help but respond. It was a beautiful day, and the prospect of riding was simply too inviting for her to resist.

She and Adam had behaved so seriously with one another for the past two weeks that it was a relief to be smiling, sharing something more than the detached professional relationship that had been established that first morning in the studio and had endured ever since.

"So why did it take you so long to follow up on his suggestion?" Her expression was stern, but there were golden highlights dancing in her eyes.

"We made a deal, remember? Nothing personal until the modeling was over."

"That did make my work a lot easier," Lysandra conceded.

"At least one of us found it easy," Adam teased. "Personally, I found it damned difficult to stand stark naked in front of a woman who stayed totally composed while she surveyed every inch of me."

She turned her full attention toward the mare, afraid to let Adam see the fiery blush she felt glowing on her cheeks. Composed? Hardly! That first day she'd had to force herself to remain unmoved. Wouldn't he gloat if he knew how many of her nights had been spent in agony recalling every line of his body or slept away in erotic dreams of him. She wasn't about to let him know how hard she had had to concentrate on staying detached from the feelings that pervaded her body each time he had stepped out from behind that screen.

She stole a glance at him and was relieved to see that he was tying the saddlebags and a rolled blanket on to his saddle. She began getting acquainted with her mount, talking softly to the pretty mare and gently stroking her velvety neck.

"My sister named her Scheherazade because she's an Arabian but we call her Schar. She's pretty well-mannered and only needs a light touch, so don't rein her in too tight, Lys. She might fight you if you do." Adam came up behind her, standing so close that she could smell the faint fragrance of the light aftershave he always wore. His hands were on her waist, and he was helping her in the saddle before she could inform him that she was perfectly capable of mounting by herself. He knew what she had been thinking but said nothing, simply handed her the reins and efficiently adjusted her stirrups.

It took her a few moments to acclimate herself to the hard saddle, pressing her legs against the mare's sides to forestall the nervous quarter-pivot the horse made as she got used to the weight of a rider. She gave the mare a light nudge with her knees and was gratified that the horse instantly responded. Adam suggested she ride around the stable yard a few times before they left the paddock, and Lysandra could feel his gaze sliding over her as she reaccustomed herself to riding. She was glad to find that, like riding a bicycle, the skill came back quickly despite the time that had passed since she'd last been on a horse.

On her final round, she was startled to notice that Adam's eyes were following the movement of her breasts as she rocked in the saddle. Sensing her awareness, he swiftly shuttered his desire-laden eyes by tipping his hat over his forehead. Seconds later, he'd swung his long frame onto the roan and was issuing a softly spoken command. He guided his mount abreast of hers and pointed toward the foothills, giving the prancing stallion his head as he galloped out of the yard; then he reined in sharply, waiting for her to catch up.

With little persuasion, her mare fell in behind the stallion, content to follow leisurely in his wake. Adam was having a little difficulty keeping the stallion reined in; the powerful animal was making it perfectly clear that he longed to run. After a few moments of struggling with him, Adam called over his shoulder, "I'm going to race this fellow toward that stand of aspens up there. He's full of it this morning. You can race along with us or just follow along. Schar will do whatever you want, but this guy's about to pull my arms from their sockets." Without waiting for an answer, he turned in the saddle and gave his mount its head.

The two were off across the flat expanse toward the foothills beyond, the long legs of the thoroughbred stretching to cover the space as if he were in a race. Speed was in his blood, and he strained to challenge the wind. His gleaming mane and tail spun out, and he moved as if free of any rider.

At the stallion's first burst of speed, the mare perked up her ears and quickened her stride before settling back in the slow trot that her training dictated she maintain until indicated otherwise. Envying the exhilaration that Adam must be feeling, and feeling confident in her returning skill, Lysandra tightened her knees and gave Schar a little kick with her heels.

The mare responded instantly, as if she had been waiting for the command, and sped after the stallion. Her shorter legs didn't cover the distance as rapidly as the thoroughbred's, but the sleek little horse gave a good accounting of herself and she and Lysandra arrived at the grove not long after Adam and his stallion.

Lysandra's hat had flown off her head and was bouncing against her shoulders when she reined in. The wind had loosened some of her hair, and she wished now she had left it down so that she could have felt the wind blowing through it as wild and free as her horse's silken black mane.

With one finger, Adam pushed his hat back from his forehead and grinned. "Not bad. We've only been waiting a few seconds." There was approval in his face and tone as he eyed her rosy cheeks and tousled appearance.

"No fair," she said and laughed. "You had a head start." She leaned forward and patted her mount's neck, then commented to her horse, "We could beat them next time, girl."

"Oh, you want to make a bet on that?" Adam challenged.

Lysandra conferred with her horse, "What d'ya think, Schar? Can we beat those two big bruisers?" As if in answer the little mare raised her head and seemed to assess her opponents with large, long-lashed eyes. Lysandra laughed and announced, "We're ready to take you on after we've rested."

Adam's deep rumbling laughter filled the quiet

grove. "So we're two bruisers, huh? For that I get to think of the prize when we beat you." He raised his brows and ran his eyes up and down her body. "I can think of any number of things I might like to claim."

"You . . . you're awfully sure you'll win," Lysandra blustered. "Do I get the same privileges if I win?" Two could play at this game, and she returned the survey. She was instantly sorry when his grin broadened and he quickly agreed, saying that he would probably enjoy whatever she claimed as her victory spoils. Oh Lord, what have I gotten myself into? she wailed inwardly.

He guided his horse closer until he was beside her. Reaching over, he crammed her hat back on her head, then surprised her by leaning forward and quickly brushing his lips across hers. Settling back, he pulled his hat down on his forehead and said, "You look right at home on that horse. I never would have guessed that you're the same sophisticated creature I met in New York. There are many sides of you, Lysandra Dillinger, and I think I'd like to know all of them."

"I could say the same about you, Adam Honour." Becoming a bit uncomfortable with the turn in the conversation, she demanded, "Are we going to sit here all morning? You promised to show me some wildlife."

And so he did, or tried to do. They rode high into the mountains, dismounting several times to look at the view. They hiked deep into the forested slopes, stretching out silently, crawling on their stomachs on the forest floor to watch a doe and her young fawn who lay almost entirely camouflaged beneath a spreading pine. Unable to get very close to the animals, Adam produced a pair of high-powered binoculars, and she stored the image of the deer in her mind so that she could sketch them later. She'd been afraid to move or to open her sketch pad for fear the graceful creatures would disappear into the forest. Her camera had lain useless by her side for even the soft whirring would have frightened them away.

Later in the morning she had more success when he guided her to a small pond where a pair of beavers were actively building their house. She was able to use her camera to film the beavers industriously gnawing down young trees and dragging them into the water. When they were discovered by nature's sentinel, the jay, and a loud squawked warning was sounded, the great tail of the larger beaver slapped the water, and the two furry animals disappeared beneath the surface of the pond.

The forest was alive with many species of birds, and Lysandra managed to get several feet of film of nuthatches, magpies and rosy finches, all busy securing food for their young. It was summer and the creatures of nature were paired off and completing the cycle of renewing life.

Adam chose a small clearing for lunch. The horses were unsaddled for the break and tethered to graze. A gurgling stream meandered down the rocky cliff at one side, and the horses took full advantage of the snow-fed waters and the lush grasses that grew on its banks.

He spread the blanket and placed the saddles down on the edge, providing them with backrests while they hungrily devoured their lunch. A chick-aree chattered at them from the high lodgepole pine overhead as they ate. "I think he's trying to tell us we're not welcome," Adam offered as he eyed the noisy little animal.

"We've disturbed his paradise," Lysandra agreed and then groaned when she moved her legs. The muscles in her backside were protesting from the unaccustomed hours she'd spent in the saddle. She rolled over on her stomach to relieve the agony and rubbed her abused behind.

"Uh oh, you're going to be one sore lady by the time we get back. I'm sorry, Lys. I forgot how painful it can be if you're not used to riding." His expression was sincerely regretful, and she grimaced a smile.

"It's not your fault. I didn't think about it either. I was so anxious to enjoy this beautiful country once we got going. I think I'd better take a rain check on seeing any more today and just suffer the ride back to the ranch." Stretching her legs again, she moaned, "Ahh, on second thought I may walk back."

Adam opened the wine and offered her a cup. "Here, maybe you can numb yourself. It's a long walk down the mountain."

"Not a good suggestion," she said, giggling as she

reached for the cup of wine. "If I drank enough not to feel any aches and pains, I'd fall off my horse." She took a sip of the chilled Rhine wine that had been stowed in a clay cooler. Eyeing the collapsible cup, she raised it toward him in a toast. "Your crystal may not be the finest, but your vintage is *magnifique*."

"Thank you, ma'am. We try out here." He drawled his words in an exaggerated Western twang. They laughed together, something they had done a lot of that morning. Lysandra enjoyed this more carefree Adam. He hadn't scowled at her, nor had he made any advances since the quick kiss and the suggestive challenge he had thrown at her at the beginning of their ride.

She took a few more sips of her wine, then rested her head on her arms and closed her eyes. Images of Adam flashed through her mind, and she recalled the way his broad back looked as he rode ahead of her, the way his eyes danced, his quick smile, and his patient identification of the birds they had seen that morning. It had been a peaceful time with him. She had loved the companionship they had shared, and loved him for it.

Loved! She tensed her body as the cold realization spread over her that it was something far more than physical attraction she felt for Adam. The Adam who had guided her up the mountain this morning had behaved like a friend, and she'd relaxed and enjoyed every minute of their excursion.

He could be so stormy, so passionate, and yet

enjoy the antics of the angry little pine squirrel, the beauty of the gentle deer and the industry of the beavers. She opened her eyes and looked across the blanket at him and was surprised to see that he had propped his head in one hand and was carefully watching her.

9

~~~~~~~~~~~~

Lysandra's body warmed with the intensity of Adam's gaze. How could blue be such a hot color? Those eyes, which had pierced her with shards of ice for days, now heated her as if they were consuming flames. "Maybe we'd better get back." She turned her head away from him and pushed up from the blanket, but every part of her body protested, and she fell back to the blanket with a groan.

Adam closed the distance between them and knelt beside her, his hands closing over her shoulders. She tried to squirm away from him, but he ordered, "Lie still, you're in no condition to get back on that horse." To make sure she couldn't escape his ministrations, he straddled her legs and continued his firm massage. "What I ought to do is throw you in the water over there."

Her struggles were renewed in earnest. "What?"

He continued moving his hands over her body while he answered her question with a laugh. "No, I don't plan on drowning you in the stream. There's a warm mineral spring just beyond those outcroppings. The heat would help your body far more than my massage." He moved away from her, and when she turned over to look at him, she saw that his shirt was already unbuttoned and loose from his pants. "I plan on enjoying it, too," he declared. "Come on, I'll race you in."

"You must be crazy! I'm not taking off my clothes in front of you!"

"Why? I did for you!"

"But . . . but that was different. I was sketching you. I'm an artist, and you were my model." She knew she was babbling, desperately trying to think of a counter-argument to his inviting suggestion. The warm mineral water would soothe her aching body, but what would sharing that pool with a nude Adam do to her nerves?

He went on removing his clothing. His boots and socks swiftly joined his shirt, and he stood up, his fingers at his belt buckle. "If you'll feel more comfortable, bring your sketch pad. Maybe *Man of Glory* can be posed in a pool of water."

His thumbs were in the elastic band of his briefs by the time he took a menacing step toward her. "If you don't get out of those clothes, I'll take them off for you," he growled, but there was a mischievous glint in his eyes. "Turnabout's fair play. I sat on that damned bench for a week while you ran those big brown eyes over all of me."

"I . . . it wasn't like that. I was interested in the planes and angles . . . ah . . . not the whole. I . . ."

"Whatever you want to call it, I'm sure your planes, angles *and* curves are just as interesting." He moved to stand over her, and she looked up the magnificent length of him to see the challenging glitter in his eyes. "Are you waiting for some help to get out of those clothes?"

He bent toward her, and she rolled across the blanket, away from his seeking hands. "Okay. Okay!" she cried desperately. "I'll do it myself, but turn your back."

"Lys, you're being ridiculous."

"No, I'm not. I provided a screen for you, the least you can do is turn your back."

"I'll wait for you in the pool." He gave up the tormenting game and walked away.

Lysandra fled behind a large shrub, and by the sound of Adam's movements behind her, she knew he had removed his last scrap of clothing and gone into the water. She unbuttoned her blouse with trembling fingers and pulled off her boots and socks. After her jeans, only her bra and underpants remained, and she considered leaving them on to offer at least some covering. On viewing the lacy garments, however, she decided that once wet they would provide next to no concealment. Besides, she could almost hear Adam reminding her that she hadn't allowed *him* to wear a pair of briefs in the studio.

The undergarments were discarded, and she hoped she wasn't blushing as she gamely made her way to the water. This is the twentieth century, she reminded herself. We're both adults, and we've both seen the nude form before.

She slipped into the water and slid as far as she could beneath the surface, relieved to see that Adam's eyes were closed. He was lounging opposite her, completely relaxed, his tanned face turned toward the sun, his golden brown body stretched out in the shallow pool.

"You've won," Lysandra stated softly when he said nothing. Thinking he might have fallen asleep, she spoke louder. "I'm here."

"I know, I could feel the ripples." He opened one eye and acknowledged her presence before stretching his arms along the bank and leaning his head back, once again the picture of relaxation.

Ignoring the innuendo, she willed her body to relax. It was a small pool, not much larger than a hot tub, and their bodies could easily touch without her having to move more than inches. She tried to settle herself on the smooth bottom.

"Admit it, it feels good," he prodded drowsily.

"Yes it does." Indeed, the water felt heavenly. She had expected that it would be only tepid, but instead it was as warm as a bath, almost hot. She could feel the heat seeping into her body, working wonders on her stiff muscles and especially her sore bottom.

"The only thing this place lacks is a whirlpool effect to be nature's own jacuzzi," Adam drawled.

"Mmm." She relaxed against the edge, finding a

smooth rock to recline against. The warm water, and the exertion of the morning, combined with the amount of wine she had consumed at lunch, drained her of all energy. She leaned her head against the soft grass-covered bank, closed her eyes and enjoyed floating buoyantly in the mineral-laden water. The soft rustling of the wind through the tops of the tall lodgepole pines lulled her to sleep.

She awoke from a delicious dream to the sensation of Adam's arm around her waist and one of his hands sliding up her legs. "Don't." She moved languid limbs, attempting to shift away from him, but her body didn't answer her brain's orders fast enough, and his mouth swooped down to claim hers.

His lips moved slowly over hers; the tip of his tongue enticed her lips open, but he didn't take complete possession of her mouth as he had always done in the past. Instead, he teased her, darting his tongue against the tip of hers, then moving it back to glide across the inside of her lips. All the while his large hands roved across her back and stomach.

Instinctively, Lysandra leaned closer. Her fingertips made forays through the dampened hairs across the hard pectoral muscles that she had sketched during the day and dreamed about every night. Her palms rested against the tightening peaks of his flat male nipples, then slid to his sides and around and across the muscles of his back. She shifted in his arms, bringing herself even closer to his body, pressing against him, her nipples brushing his chest.

With a deep groan, Adam intensified the kiss. His tongue, no longer teasing but filling her mouth, touched every part of the sensitive recess, then trailed across her cheek to her neck.

His hands tightened around her waist, and in a swift motion he was beneath her. She was stretched out, floating atop his body while he placed tantalizing nibbles down her throat and across the swelling of her breasts. "You have no planes and angles," he murmured between kisses. "Only curves. The sweetest curves ever created."

He slid her body higher until his mouth closed over the nipple of one breast, his tongue encircling as his lips laved the tender aureole. Its twin was treated to identical pleasure, and Lysandra arched against him, reveling in the hardness of his body against hers. Her hands slid up from his shoulders, and she buried her long fingers in his hair. The golden strands, heated by the sun and the water, curled silkily around her fingers.

"Lys, Lys. I want you," he murmured against her skin and, in one movement, swept her up and rose from the shallow pool. The urgency in his voice and the cooler air blowing against her heated body sounded warning bells within her. How could she have let herself get so far out of control? She couldn't let this go on. There could be disastrous results, results that would bring misery to everyone involved.

She stiffened her body and tried to stretch her feet to the ground. "No, Adam. We can't." Her soft protest sounded unconvincing even to her own ears.

"You're not saying no now, Lys. I want you and I'm going to have you. I need you," he said with utter conviction. They reached the blanket, and he let her body slide down his, keeping her locked close to him as his arms wound tightly around her. He silenced her low whimper by covering her mouth, his tongue invading, parrying with hers, dueling until she lost the battle and returned his invasion. Tremors coursed through her as he moved back and forth against her, his moist chest barely touching her aroused nipples. One of his thighs insinuated itself between hers, and the swaying motion was continued until the soft cries emitting from her throat told him that she was no longer resisting the need he had built within her.

They dropped together to the blanket, lying on their sides, their arms and legs intertwined. His large hand moved over her wet body, the water droplets clinging to the smooth surface and aiding the fluid motion as he caressed her hip, and continued up the inside of her thighs until the heel of his hand rested at their juncture and began a rocking movement that sent her last reservation fluttering away with the mountain breeze.

His mouth released hers and crossed her face until he reached her fragile earlobe where his teeth gently nibbled at the tender skin before the tip of his tongue began exploring the delicate folds of her ear, renewing the tremors that had overtaken her body. When he grazed the very core of her throbbing womanhood with his fingertips, Lysandra instinctively tightened her thighs. Her inexperienced body wanted but shied away from the fulfillment his fingers promised.

Adam returned his lips to hers, his tongue invading at the same moment that his fingers slipped inside her. With tongue and fingers, he overwhelmed her senses, stroking until she knew nothing but the craving drive to be part of him.

"You're so tight, so perfect." His words were gasped between his ragged breaths. "Now, Lys."

He covered her and settled between her thighs with a tender escalation of masculine power. She could feel the heated hardness of him surging against her and knew she wanted him to possess her more than anything she'd ever wanted. This glorious man had haunted her dreams, had caressed her body in those dreams, but never in all her fantasies had she responded like this. The reality of the man was so much greater than the fantasy. Her love for him stoked her passion, and she eagerly raised her hips to meet him, offering what she'd never given another.

Adam entered her swiftly but hesitated until her body accommodated his, then he began a pulsating cadence within her. His slow thrusts accelerated until she was clinging to him while wave upon wave of sensation sent her soaring above the high mountains, soaring to some place that only this man could take her. She cried out his name, and her shudders merged with his as they reached the summit together.

Planting soft, moist kisses across her cheeks and burying his face in her neck, Adam moved to his side, taking her with him. Cradled against his big body, Lysandra felt safe and secure. She wanted to shout that she loved him. She remembered his words of encouragement, the tender compliments he had murmured as he took her, and she cherished each one until she also recalled that there had been no words of love. Chilled by the realization that he had finally achieved what he wanted from her— satisfied his desire without offering his love—she started to move away.

"No. Stay right where you are," he growled sensually against her hair. "Are you all right? Did I hurt you?"

"No." He hadn't hurt her physically. His lovemaking had been wonderful, beyond her imagination. But emotionally? What if he rejected the love she yearned to offer? She didn't dare become vulnerable to that kind of pain.

Adam rolled her gently onto her back, imprisoning her with his arms and chest. "You've never unleashed all that passion before, have you?" She stared up into his face, not knowing how to answer. Would he laugh at her admission that he'd been the first? Was he expecting hysterics? Demands of marriage in exchange for "ruining her" as if they were protagonists in some Victorian novel? She turned her head slowly from side to side, and a tear spilled from the corner of each eye. He kissed the glistening droplet away, which only prompted more to fall. "Don't cry, Lys. You were wonderful. Next time it will be even better, I promise."

"No, Adam. There can't be another time. I can't risk . . ." She couldn't put her feelings into words.

"If you're worried about repercussions," he assured her tenderly, "I'll take care of you. Chances are we won't have anything to worry about this time, but we won't gamble again. I would've been prepared had I known you were a virgin. You should have . . ."

"You planned this?" White-faced, she cut off his sentence.

"No, honey." Adam's tone was softly indulgent. "I didn't plan this. I really tried to play by your rules, but I couldn't stand it any longer. I've gone half-crazy wanting you." He lowered his head and began nuzzling her neck, placing tiny kisses along its slender length until he buried his face in her hair.

"Out of love or just lust?" She twisted away from the lips that were tantalizing her and glared up at him.

"It wasn't lust, Lys. I'm sure of that," he vowed. "It was very special. I want you in my bed tonight and every night from now on. One taste isn't going to be enough for me."

She caught his face in her hands before he could kiss her again. "For how long? Until you've satisfied your craving? I can't live with you like that, not knowing how long it will last."

"We can't take out insurance, but the way I feel now it could last a lifetime. Stay with me, Lys, don't go back to New York." His voice was ragged.

"What are you saying?"

"That you live with me, be my mistress. You can't deny that you enjoyed my lovemaking, that if I touched you again, you wouldn't go wild in my arms."

"No, I may not be able to deny that, but I won't be your mistress!" she cried, her dark eyes glazing in torment. "Let me up!"

This time he released her, and she raced to where her clothing lay in a heap on the forest floor. When she was fully clothed she emerged from her make-shift dressing room behind a shrub to find Adam dressed and picking up the remains of their lunch. He angrily stuffed everything into the saddlebags.

She crossed to her saddle and prepared to lift it, needing to hurry things along. He grabbed her arm and spun her around to face him, his blue eyes flaming. "We're not finished."

Her defiant glare made him swear under his breath. "What do you want from me, Lys? A declaration of undying love and a marriage certificate?"

She was too distraught to think and shouted, "Yes, dammit! I love you!"

She was more surprised than he by the admission but stood her ground as he flared, "Well, maybe I love you, too, but that doesn't mean I'll marry you." Finally recognizing what they'd both just said, Adam's expression softened, and he dropped his arm. "I've never said that to another woman. Let it be enough."

Tears blinded her, blurring his image as she abruptly turned away. "It's not enough," she whispered, her shoulders shaking with disappointment and pain.

Again he forced her around to face him, pulling her against his chest, but his hands were gentle as he stroked her back. "Can't you understand? Making it legal doesn't guarantee we'll stay together. It would only make everything harder if we split up. You love me, and I think I love you. That's all anyone needs. Live with me, Lys."

He pressed her head against his chest, making her painfully aware of the unsteady beat of his heart.

What he was offering wasn't anything out of the ordinary, she supposed. Wasn't that what many couples did? Well, it might be right for others, but not for her. She needed permanence, legality, a binding agreement. How could she make him understand?

She pulled her head away from his chest. Unable to look at him, she voiced her refusal to somewhere in the vicinity of his third shirt button. Her fingers toyed with the buttons absentmindedly as she searched for the words to explain. "I . . . I can't live with you under those circumstances. There's no future in it. I need more than just your love. I want it all, Adam—name, family, children."

"You want me, Lys." He shifted his weight, and his thighs pressed against hers. "I'm offering you all I can. Maybe I've rushed you again." He tilted her chin up, and she was forced to meet his gaze. His eyes were tender with desire for her, but at the first tentative touch of his lips, the tenderness changed to fiery possession. All her newly awakened desires were rekindled and burned through her veins. She responded by wrapping her arms around his waist and pulling him closer, returning the deep kiss until their harsh breathing blended. Adam released her slowly, but kept his hands on her forearms to balance her. "Remember how it feels, Lys. Are you willing to let it go?"

He dropped his hands away from her and turned

toward the horses. She stood gulping in the fresh pine-scented air, trying to prevent herself from calling him back. She wanted to fling herself into his arms, promise him anything, but years of hiding her true feelings protected her. She busied herself rolling up the blanket and was soon ready for the ride back to the ranch.

The trail down the mountain was different but equally beautiful as the one they had taken earlier in the day. This time, Lysandra was not completely enthralled by the creatures and scenery they passed. Gone was the camaraderie they had shared earlier. Adam didn't stop or point out things of interest as he had done that morning. He didn't speak at all.

Once back at the ranch, she dismounted and fled to the safety of the house, needing to get away from him. It was torture to keep from remembering the feel of his powerful body surging against hers. She needed to be alone, if only for a few hours, to fortify her resolve not to succumb to the need he aroused in her.

Once inside the house, she headed directly for her room, but Clayton was waiting for her in the hallway. "Did you enjoy yourself, Lys? It was a great day to go riding."

Attempting to mask her inner turmoil, she answered levelly, stealthily averting her eyes. "It was wonderful. I'm really tired, Clayton. Will you excuse me if I go lie down for a while?"

Clayton was much too astute not to notice the slight quiver of her lower lip and her overbright dark eyes. "Something's wrong," he stated emphatically.

"Come with me. You know you can talk to me, and it looks like you need to talk to somebody."

His concern was her undoing, and she meekly allowed him to escort her across the living room and into the study where he closed the door behind them. Gently guiding her to a couch, he sat down beside her and reached for her hand. "We're friends, aren't we?"

"Of course," Lysandra said, thinking that Adam's father was probably the last person she should be talking to about her personal problems, but he refused to let the matter drop. "You've got the same look Sharon used to have when she needed to talk but tried to head to her room and cry it out. She was sure it was the end of the world until she discovered that a problem shared was not nearly so heavy." Patting her hand he prodded, "I'm pretty experienced at listening."

"It's Adam." She lowered her lashes, unable to make the declaration to Clayton's face. "I'm in love with him."

"I see." Clayton said the two simple words containing a wealth of compassion. Looking up, she met his gaze, saw the sympathetic lines that creased his mouth and realized that he had already known of her feelings; had known, too, that she would suffer because of them.

"He . . . Adam wants me to stay here and live with him." She couldn't bear to tell Clayton what had prompted his son's offer, but wanted him to know how she felt. She needed to tell someone who understood Adam far better than she did.

"But . . . he doesn't want to marry me." She blinked back the tears that gathered in her eyes. "I can't do that, Clayton. I just can't."

"Perhaps you can, Lys." Clayton cleared his throat as if he were somewhat shocked with himself for being able to say such a thing. Aware of her astonishment, a slight tinge of pink crept up his cheek, but he didn't retreat from his surprising position. "I'm almost certain Adam loves you, too, Lys. I know you're the best thing that's ever happened to him, and I was kind of hoping I could count on you to get past that wall of bitterness he's built up inside him since Marian walked out. I realize you're not the kind of woman who'd find it easy to share a man's life without the contract that makes it acceptable in society's eyes, but perhaps you'll change your mind if you hear me out."

"Clayton, I . . ."

"Please, Lys. Listen to me," Clayton pleaded, his rough tone implying that it was going to be as difficult for him to explain what he meant as it might be for her to understand.

"All right." Lysandra brushed her hand over her eyes and composed herself. "But I don't think that I can do what Adam's asking. I know what can happen when people don't accept full responsibility for their actions."

Nodding his head, Clayton looked down at his shoes as the words began slowly. "Adam was thirteen when my wife left me. The two of them were very close. Adam adored her. Like so many boys that age, he had her way up on a pedestal. Marian wasn't strong enough to face him when she decided to leave. I've found it very hard to forgive her for that, but eventually I understood. Adam never did understand, and before you came, I didn't think he'd ever allow another woman to become that important to him."

He passed a shaky hand over his mouth before continuing, "He's never given his heart, only taken what a man in his position is offered. He's had women here, Lys, I can't deny it, but not one of them was like you."

Lysandra couldn't help herself; she shook her head in denial. "He hasn't offered me anything more than he gave to the others. How different does that make me?"

Clayton looked directly into her tear-moistened eyes. "Very different," he insisted gruffly. "None of them were asked to share his life in any way other than a brief affair. I know my son, and he wouldn't make an offer like the one he's made you unless he expected it to last. He's afraid of that piece of paper, but he's given you all he's got to give and that's his love. I can't tell you how grateful I am to you for showing him he's still able to care. Wait for him, Lys," Clayton urged. "He'll come around and do it right. All he needs is time. Trust comes hard for some people, and Adam's had good reason to doubt its existence."

Lysandra couldn't doubt Clayton's sincerity, but she wasn't convinced that all he said applied to her and Adam. "I don't know if I can live like that." She clasped her hands together, paling when she heard the sound of the kitchen door opening and of Adam's familiar long stride passing down the hall on the way to his room.

"Afraid of what others might think?"

"That's part of it." Lysandra's mind raced with the implications of living with Adam as his mistress. She had been born illegitimate. Would this be so different? She'd be an illegitimate wife. Could she live without Adam no matter what the circumstances?

"Follow your heart, Lys." Clayton stood up and held out his hand to her, sensing that there was nothing more he could say to convince her but needing to offer one last argument to make his case. "Be honest with yourself. I think you need Adam's love as much as he needs yours. I can feel the emptiness in you that disappears whenever he walks into the room. You can help heal the wounds his mother made and heal your own as well. Believe me, I'd consider myself lucky accepting you into our family, with or without the formalities."

Deeply moved by Clayton's kindness and his honesty, Lysandra didn't know what to say. Impulsively, she gave him her hand, and when he pulled her to her feet, she awkwardly wrapped her arms around him and gave him a clumsy hug. "Adam is lucky to have you. You're a special man, Clayton, and I thank you."

"Think on it, Lys." Clayton's eyes softened as he watched the play of conflicting emotions cross her face. "Whatever happens, you'll always have me for a friend. Now, why don't you go and get some rest like you planned? I'll see you at dinner."

Following Clayton's orders, Lysandra made her way to her room, grateful that she didn't run into Adam along the way. She entered the bathroom and filled the tub, pouring in a generous amount of fragrant herbal bubblebath before easing her sore body into the water. She began to relax until, like a running film, the events of the afternoon replayed in her head.

The bathroom receded, and she reclined once more in that isolated spring enclosed within a small forest glade. The herbal-scented water filling her nostrils became the scent of the forest, combined with the masculine tang of her lover's skin.

Clayton had said that her love could heal Adam's wounds; she wondered if it might be possible for their relationship to heal her own. Would living with Adam help either of them? Would Adam change his opinion of marriage as Clayton predicted? If she decided against becoming Adam's mistress, could she forget him and go on with her life?

The unanswerable questions repeated themselves in her mind until she laid back against the edge of the tub, forcing her thoughts away from the source of her turmoil to that safe place she had constructed years ago to counteract her pain. She was filled with distress to discover that her familiar haven was no longer available to her; her inner sanctuary was filled with the unwavering figure of a man. Adam was inside her and he refused to be vanquished; he wouldn't allow her to escape.

She slipped lower into the cooling water, her lashes fanning down to staunch the flow of tears that wouldn't stop. She tried to muffle her sobs by burying her face in the washcloth, but nothing helped as she cried out the grief she'd carried since childhood and her fear over what lay ahead.

10

~~~~~~~~~~~~~~~

There'll be no more of this, Lys." Adam's voice was a harsh command as he strode into the bathroom. Moving with lightning speed, he hauled her shivering body up and out of the tub. Lysandra was too shocked by his presence in the room to do anything but gape at him. He swiftly enclosed her dripping body in her terrycloth robe and began roughly toweling her dry.

"What the hell are you trying to do to yourself, catch pneumonia?" he demanded vehemently, his eyes stormy until he saw that her teeth were chattering. Scooping her up in his arms, he carried her through to the bedroom, tore a blanket from her bed, then enveloped her in it until all that remained showing was her face.

"Adam . . . you shouldn't be in here," she managed to say between the shudders that were slowly dissipating beneath the warmth of the blanket. Ignoring her protests, he sat down on the bed, cradling her on his lap while his hands briskly rubbed up and down over the heavy material that covered her.

"I've been very patient with you, lady." Adam tightened his grip on her when she would have squirmed away. "I've let you stay inside that shell you've developed long enough. Tonight it ends! I'm not going to let you tear yourself apart while I sit in the next room and listen." A renewed vehemence brought on by frustration sounded in his voice. "You'll tell me what's troubling you or so help me I'll . . . I'll . . ."

She stared into his worried blue eyes. He cared! He cared or he wouldn't be raging at her as if he'd like to wring her neck. Tentatively, her lips curved upwards in a smile, the fight gone out of her as she found the love she was seeking reflected in Adam's face. "You'll what?" she asked softly, her wet lashes and tear-stained cheeks making her look entirely too vulnerable for him to respond aggressively to her challenge.

With surprising strength, Adam kept her atop his lap as he scooted himself to the head of the bed, lifting her up, then seating her beside him. He leaned back against the headboard and stretched his legs out alongside hers. Without looking at her, he took a deep breath and released it, staring up at the ceiling as he slowly began speaking. "Sometimes when I look at you I can feel what you're feeling. I know you've been hurt and I want to know how. You said it wasn't another man, but something is keeping you from me, and it's killing me not knowing what it is."

Responding to his raw tone, Lysandra lifted her hand and placed it over his lips. She could see that it was time to tell him what was preventing her from giving herself fully. It was a new experience for her to have someone else ache because she was hurting, and she couldn't help herself. She placed her head upon his shoulder, lovingly dropped her palm over his heart and waited for the last quiver of cold to desert her body.

At first, she had difficulty getting the words past her lips, but when he remained silent, encouraging her by covering her hand with his and tenderly caressing her soft palm, she gathered confidence and told him everything about herself, beginning with the day she had discovered that she was illegitimate and ending with her eighteenth birthday, the day she had left the last of her foster homes and the last in the long line of families that hadn't cared enough to want her to stay.

"I care, Lys. I want you to stay." Adam shifted his body, lowering his shoulder to lean over her. He gave her a kiss on the cheek, a gentle kiss that told her he understood, that he loved her.

"I know," she replied, moved by his protectiveness, but still uncertain. "But don't you see how hard it is for me to give myself totally to you when I've no proof that it will last?

"What if I got pregnant, Adam? I'd rather die than bring another child into the world who would have no one to call her own."

"You'd never give up a child of yours like your mother did," Adam stated fiercely, as if he needed to convince himself more than her. She felt the change in him and debated whether or not to tell him that she knew what had occurred between him and his mother. She opened her mouth to say something that would convince him that, although she wouldn't give up his child, the child would still suffer—would never really belong. He prevented her from speaking by stating forcefully, "But that issue won't come up. It'll be just you and me, sweetheart. I'll make sure there are no children."

"You don't want a family?" Lysandra asked, swallowing the sudden ache parching her throat. She'd always yearned for a family, a close-knit group of people who would love and protect one another, but it seemed the only man she wanted didn't have the same kind of dreams.

His handsome features suddenly hardened. "Not for me," he answered. "And now I've found a woman who feels the same way. Neither of us will bring pain to some unsuspecting child. If we should eventually decide to go our separate ways, no one will get hurt."

A long silence settled around them. Lysandra felt bruised, exhausted from the purge of emotion that had occurred in the bath and unable to confront him on anything that might bring on another session of shattering sobs.

Knowing her past, Adam felt sure she'd not want to chance producing a family. Like him, she was aware of what could happen if the relationship didn't last. The torment she'd experienced when she'd discovered that no one cared about her had been painful and deep, so similar to the feelings he'd suffered when his mother had deserted him.

Aware that she was physically and emotionally spent, he decided not to dwell on what was still left unsaid between them. "You, my sweet, need something warm in your stomach. I'm going out to the kitchen to make you something to eat, and I want you to get under those covers and stay there."

"You don't have to do that." She didn't move, watching him roll off the bed and get to his feet. "I can get dressed for dinner."

"Not necessary," he informed her lightly. "I sent Dad over to Betty's so we could have some time to ourselves. Since you're in no shape to cook, I'm going to make dinner and serve it in here." He walked through the door, calling back over his shoulder. "I've cooked for you before. Get into bed and let me wait on you."

"Isn't it my turn?" she called back, surprised that her legs still held her as she got off the bed and walked to the chest of drawers that held her night clothes.

"I'm sure I'll think up some way for you to pay me back." Adam's voice drifted away as he neared the kitchen.

She smiled at his suggestive tone and opened a drawer to pull out the long pink satin nightgown she hadn't yet worn. She'd slept each night in an over-sized T-shirt, but if she were going to be joined by Adam for dinner, she had to wear something more glamorous, something that would cover her bare legs. A blush came over her when she realized that he'd already seen all there was to see on more than one occasion. Seeing her reflection in the mirror, she noted that her legs were just about all the gown covered.

It seemed to take an inordinately long time before she heard him walking back down the hall toward her room. She'd spent the time brushing her hair to an ebony sheen and applying a small amount of lipstick and blusher to her pale features. When he walked into the room, she was sitting up in bed with the covers pulled to her waist.

His low whistle of appreciation brought an answering smile of pleasure to her lips. "You like it?" she asked, knowing full well that the gown didn't really cover anything, merely enhancing what was barely concealed by the pink satin and lace. Maybe Adam didn't share all her dreams for the future, but tonight she didn't care. Tonight she would forget about everything but the man she loved.

"It's a damned shame that I'm starving, or I'd insist you pay for your meal in advance." He approached and placed the large tray he carried down on the bedside table. He lifted a linen napkin and unfolded it, then gave it a flourishing wave and announced grandly, "Dinner is served, madam." The formality of his pose was ruined when he ordered, "Move over, honey. I'm starved."

With amazing ease, he kicked off his shoes and climbed in beside her, frowning pointedly as she tried to readjust herself against the second pillow and to rearrange the covers. "Settled?" he asked impatiently, and at the slightly offended lift of her brows, directed her to stop moving around so that he could pass her a plate.

The cheese omelet, his specialty it seemed, was done to perfection and accompanied by thick slices of Virginia ham and broiled tomatoes. They ate the simple meal on fine white china with heavy silver flatware. Few words were spoken. Finally, Lysandra had eaten the last morsel on her plate, and Adam had poured champagne into two delicate crystal glasses.

"I'm impressed," she complimented truthfully. "But aren't you overdoing things a bit with the champagne?"

"Spirits are part of my plan to help you get some rest. Where's the rule that says it can't be champagne that lulls you to sleep?"

"Seems a waste of such an expensive drink," she teased, taking a sip of the fine vintage and crinkling her nose as the heady bubbles fizzled softly upon her upper lip.

"Nothing I do for you is a waste." He lifted one brow, his leering expression making her giggle.

Their interlude seemed bittersweet, each of them avoiding anything that might dispel the playful atmosphere Adam had painstakingly set for the remainder of the evening.

When he'd finished his wine, he replaced his empty glass on the bedside table and watched her as she took the last sip of hers. "I like what you're doing on the stallion, Lys. It already looks much more like Hurricane than the first one you did."

"Clayton showed me a picture of him." Her dark eyes glowed with the pleasure of his compliment. "I should be able to have it ready to go to the foundry in the next few days."

"Great." He folded his arms across his chest. "Dad's birthday party is scheduled for the week after next. I've arranged for you to use our plane to fly the piece to the foundry in Denver. That way, we'll be sure you'll have enough time to finish it before the party.

"I've heard from Sharon, and she and her husband will be arriving a few days early. I'm glad they're coming and bringing Marilee for Dad's birthday. It's always good to have them here for a few days."

A bit worried about Adam's sister's reaction to her presence on the ranch and her status in Adam's life, Lysandra would have said something, but she could tell that Adam didn't want to talk about anything that might dampen the light-hearted, companionable atmosphere they were enjoying. He took her empty glass and announced, "I'll take these dishes into the kitchen, then be back to tuck you in. I'll even listen to your prayers and tell you a bedtime story."

"You're making me sound like a six-year-old," Lysandra berated, sighing as the mattress dipped when he got off the bed; her languid limbs felt like sponge rubber.

By the time he returned, Lysandra was struggling to stay awake, but her eyelids were far too heavy. The champagne had done its job, dulling her senses until she felt like she was floating in a sea of warm mist.

"Lys?" Adam's low murmur got little response. Only a tender smile appeared at the sound of his voice, but he acted on that small sign of acceptance. His clothes landed soundlessly on the carpeted floor beside the bed. Getting added reassurance from her unprotesting moves to accommodate him as he slid beneath the covers, he smiled down at her as he reached up to switch off the lamp.

Breathing deeply, he savored the smooth feel of satin brushing the bare skin of his thigh. "Adam?" Lysandra murmured sleepily, fitting her soft curves against him. Her breath whispered over the hair on his chest, and he slid his arm beneath her, gathering her tightly into the shelter of his arms.

"I'm here," he whispered, fighting the urge to make passionate love to her even though she was seconds away from necessary sleep. He couldn't prevent his muffled groan when he realized she'd been asleep all along, feeling the slight movements of her limbs as she made herself comfortable, her hand resting lifelessly upon his flat stomach.

Many hours later, when a thin gray light announced the gathering dawn, Lysandra came awake to the feel of her satin gown gliding sensually down her bare legs. Warm hands slid over her smooth skin, following the path of the receding satin until it was swept away over her ankles. Immediately thereafter, those hands traversed her nakedness from thigh to hip to breast, making her moan with delight. Each enticing stroke Adam made was calculated to bring the most intense reaction. He tormented her breasts with the gentle lashing of his tongue, and any control she might have tried to call upon was far beyond her reach.

His fingers were partners in the erotic dance of his mouth, molding the fevered flesh for the delectation of his tongue. Unbearable heat consumed her as he released the soft fullness his hands had cupped to smooth down her ribcage to her stomach, where one rhythmically circled her navel while the other skimmed lower.

His featherlight caresses brought wild cries of joy from her parted lips. "Adam. . . . Oh, Adam." She panted his name, arching against the hand that was expertly coaxing a hot rush of bliss from her writhing body.

Unashamedly, she twisted with uncontrolled response when his lips arrived on hers to enhance her pleasure, his tongue darting in unison with his stroking fingertips. Whatever she had to give belonged to him, but the pleasure was too much for her to sustain without giving it back. She reached for him, seeking him with hungry lips and searching hands.

He was swiftly suffering the joyful agony of his own need, his heartbeats thundering beneath the delicate flicks of her tongue across his flat nipples. Her wandering fingers slipped below his waist, trail-

ing down the soft line of hair until she found him.
She was rewarded by the thrilling knowledge of her
power to arouse him.

Adam's breath hissed through his clenched teeth
as he caught her arms and pinned her beneath him,
ravaging her mouth again and again. Not stopping
there, his body slid lower, his lips and tongue
tenderly assaulting first one breast than the other.

She sucked in her breath when his tongue trailed
lower, circling her navel before he buried his golden
head between her thighs. Crying out his name, she
shuddered to climax, only to be raised once more to
that passionate peak where nothing else existed but
the elemental hunger that had to be satisfied.

Needing her, Adam pulled her on top of him. She
was filled with him and provided all his thrusting
body required for fulfillment. As the gauzy shroud of
dawn lifted higher in the eastern sky, they created
their own glorious light, a blinding flash of pleasure
that bathed them both in its golden warmth.

Locked together, they lay motionless, spent, until
Adam shifted her to his side, recovering from the
encompassing passion that was blissfully slow to
diffuse. Lysandra's palm curled over the curve of
flesh above his heart and a tender smile curled her
lips as she felt the agonized beat slow to a steady
drumming.

"God, I'm sorry," he gritted, laying his arm across
his eyes as the harsh words fell from his lips. "I didn't
think, Lys."

A cold shaft of anxiety cut into Lysandra's heart.

Was he already having regrets? Apologizing for taking things farther than he'd intended?

"Don't you understand?" Adam pulled himself up to a half-raised position. "I didn't use any protection."

Was his tone accusatory? Lysandra couldn't bear it if it was, and her lips, still swollen from his kisses, went dry and stiff. Aching inside, unable to look at him, she pulled the discarded sheets up and over her nakedness, turning her face away.

She heard his swift intake of breath and waited with dread for what he would say next. "I'm sorry, Lys. It won't happen like this again. Don't you believe me?"

All she heard was his solemn vow not to let something so spontaneously wonderful occur in the future. Is that what their involvement would cost? A single tear wended its way down her cheek, and she lifted her hand to wipe it away.

"Don't cry, sweetheart." Adam propped himself up on his elbow and leaned over her, surveying her face. "We made a mistake, but if we're lucky, we won't have to pay for it."

She was already paying for it but didn't want him to know that, didn't want him to know that she'd already made her decision. "It doesn't matter," she whispered softly, and it didn't matter for she'd soon be gone. She didn't have the courage to tell him that their affair was over when he reached out and captured her chin in his hand, lowering his lips to hers.

"Thank God," he murmured, bestowing a gentle kiss that increased the pain of knowing she must leave him.

Lifting his mouth away from her soft lips, he used his thumb to tenderly wipe away the moisture pooling near the corner of her mouth. "We're beautiful together, Lys. More beautiful than anything I've ever known. You realize that, don't you?"

His blue eyes burned through the layer of ice that encased her soul, their tender message always capable of melting her heart. "I love you, Adam," she whispered and accepted the fierce hug he gave her for the words.

Without meaning to, her eyes devoured him as he bounded out of bed and searched the floor for the clothes he'd discarded the previous night. He caught her watching him, and his white teeth flashed in a satisfied grin, then raised his shirt over his head and pulled it down over his chest. "I have to leave you today," he informed her. "I've got to spend a couple of weeks in Denver, but I'll be home in time for Dad's party. We've got a tough engineering problem at one of the mines. I'm sorry I didn't tell you last night, but I didn't think it was a very good time."

Maybe she could leave without having to confront him with her decision! Lysandra managed to hide her relief and to convey how much she'd miss him, hating herself for her cowardice as she silently made plans to complete her work, then go back to New York without seeing him again.

"While I'm gone, you can move your things into

my room." Adam's warm expression told her he hadn't sensed her withdrawal.

"I don't know, Adam." She forced the vague statement through her tight lips, trying unsuccessfully to smile.

At first she thought he meant to argue with her, but he must have thought better of it, for he let the matter drop. He muttered something about discussing it when he returned home, then marched back to the bed and conferred a breathtaking kiss on her full lips.

The kiss was hungry and brief, but Lysandra tried to convey all the love that was contained in her heart. It was an unsatisfactory good-bye, but he seemed pleased with her passionate response for his eyes glazed with desire as he scanned the rapid movements of her breasts beneath the sheet.

With visible effort, he tore his eyes away and glanced at the clock. "I hate like hell to leave you." His brow furrowed, and he raked a hand through his hair. "I've got to go, Lys. Bob's probably already waiting for me at the airstrip. I'll call you every night, I promise."

Thinking that he'd somehow sensed her agitation, Lysandra blew him a kiss. "Don't worry about me, Adam. I'll be able to get much more work done on your father's present if you're not around. I know that you've got other responsibilities. You have your work, and I have mine."

He didn't look as if he liked her last comment, but she could tell by his hurried movements that he didn't feel he had the time to ask her what she meant by it. "I'll try to wrap it up as soon as possible." He hesitated by the door as if he wasn't sure he should leave yet knew he had to go. "You're more important to me than any gold mine, Lys."

Feeling torn apart inside, Lysandra eased his mind with a playful laugh. "But I can't compete with molybdenum. Get going, Adam. If I start now, I can be in the studio in time to catch the best light. Stop stalling."

"Yes, ma'am." His flashing grin inflicted more pain, but he didn't see the tension in her as he left the room. She listened as he entered his own bedroom and heard him drag something heavy across the wood floor. A few minutes after that she heard his bedroom door open and shut and his footsteps faded down the hall that led to the front door.

Needing to catch one last look at him, she tore out of bed, forgetful of her nudity as she ran to the window in time to see him lifting a suitcase into the back of the pickup. As if he had some sixth sense about her, he turned around and spotted her at the window. She could see the pleasure it gave him to find her watching his departure. Even at that distance, she could see the sudden light in his eyes as they dropped from her face to the rounded fullness of her exposed breasts. She saw his mouth open in a delighted laugh, but he shook his finger at her with mock disapproval, then lifted his hand to his mouth and blew her a kiss. She waved at him, draping the curtain over her bosom as she watched him climb into the truck, start the engine and place a heavy foot on the gas pedal. By the time the swirling fountains of dust produced by the truck's spinning wheels had cleared, Adam was gone, and Lysandra was left alone to contemplate her future without him. It seemed pretty bleak.

11

〜〜〜〜〜〜〜〜〜〜

The burnished metal horse gleamed in the mid-morning sun, but the red-rimmed eyes of the woman who surveyed it were shadowed and dull. Lysandra had worked feverishly for close to two weeks in order to finish Clayton's gift in time for his birthday celebration. The only respite in the dogged pace she had set for herself had occurred during the brief period of time that the mold had been flown to the foundry in Denver, but as soon as it was returned to the Bar H, she'd immediately set to work on the finishing.

Seated before the worktable in the studio, Lysandra's fingers brushed lovingly over the polished flanks she'd modeled after a magnificent animal. Tactilely, she contemplated the final chasing that had produced strong contrasts of light and dark along the textured bronze. The rendition she'd created appeared inherently savage, almost alive. By accentuating the surface to provide a rapid shift of light, she'd been able to effect an emotional violence in the pawing legs, flared nostrils and windswept mane. She knew that she'd never have been able to infuse the statue with such passion if she wasn't being torn apart by her own turbulent war of emotions.

During Adam's absence, her conviction that they had no future together had solidified like a stone inside her. His nightly phone calls had become pure torture, for she couldn't find the courage to tell him that she'd be gone before he came back to the ranch.

The arrival of Adam's sister, her husband Mark and their young daughter Marilee had further cemented her decision to leave. The small family was a prime example for Lysandra of all she would be missing if she settled for becoming a mistress instead of a wife. Although the Johnsons did their best to include her in their conversations, asking her questions about her work, Lysandra felt like an outsider and knew she always would. Sharon had relished the chance to exchange shop talk with a fellow artist, but Lysandra guessed that Adam's blond, blue-eyed sister wouldn't have been as open or friendly with her if she'd been aware of her involvement with Adam. No, she was missing the one essential ingredient that bonded their family together: love. Adam had never been able to say that he loved her without qualification. Even though he'd admitted that he *might* love her, she couldn't live without the permanent commitment those words should entail.

It was natural that during her visit Sharon and Clayton relived a countless number of happy memories, laughing over the many pranks she and Adam had pulled as children. Although Lysandra enjoyed listening to the stories, it pointed out to her more clearly than anything else ever could how important a shared family history could be. She'd never had anyone who had participated in her life long enough to forge a lasting bond, and Adam was not offering her that permanence in the future.

One evening while listening to Clayton proudly expound on the joyous birth of his granddaughter, Lysandra had experienced an inner pain so great it was almost impossible to hide it. After that, she began staying for longer periods in her studio, giving the excuse that she wanted Clayton's gift to be ready for its unveiling at the party.

For the last two days she hadn't been able to face Adam's calls, ignoring Clayton's light taps at her door until he was convinced she was asleep. In the mornings, Clayton had warned her that his son didn't approve of the overlong hours she was keeping, but she'd laughed off his concern, saying she was doing what she loved best and when immersed in her work, she lost all track of time.

Yet, even by working herself into total exhaustion, she couldn't escape the painful truth. No matter how much she loved and wanted Adam, she couldn't become his mistress. Every day she would spend with him, she'd yearn to have his child and would die a little because she'd know he didn't share that desire. She had to face the agonizing knowledge that if she ever became pregnant, something essential between them would wither and die.

Adam was due to return in two days' time, so Lysandra had to face Clayton today to tell him that she wouldn't be present for his party. She needed Clayton's help in order to leave the ranch—but how could she tell him it was because she couldn't bear to see Adam again? He would think her a coward, not good enough for his son, and perhaps he'd be right.

She had learned a painful lesson about herself, and it was one that didn't foster any pride. When Adam had told her the meaning of her name, he had seemed to be convinced that her lofty thoughts could elevate a man above the mundane things of earth; but she couldn't live up to her namesake's illustrious notability. She had discovered that it was the mundane things in life she required most to ease the loneliness she'd endured since childhood. Family, children, security and, most of all, love—she found the simple things necessary in order to nurture those transcendent thoughts that could lift anyone from the ordinary to the sublime. Look at how far her work had progressed since she'd fallen in love. Both *Man of Glory* and Clayton's horse depicted emotions never before present in her work and, at last, she felt free to display those impressions to the world. If nothing else, because of her involvement with Adam and her friendship with his father, she was no longer hiding from herself or her own feelings.

It was going to be painful to cut off her friendship with Clayton; almost as hard as it was to leave Adam.

Clayton had given her so much, and she'd no more forget him than she'd be able to disregard her love for his magnificent son. She wondered if Adam would have as much trouble forgetting her. Clayton had told her that his wife had remarried immediately after their divorce to a wealthy, older man from a socially prominent family in Boston. Adam had judged that she'd deserted them for the money and position, because his father hadn't yet accumulated the immense wealth they now enjoyed. Finally understanding why Adam had disapproved of her friendship with his father, Lysandra also realized that her desertion might serve to fortify Adam's belief that all women were disloyal and untrustworthy.

She dreaded thinking about Adam's reaction but felt she had no other choice. Two minutes with him and she knew he'd be able to convince her to stay even knowing what would eventually happen if she did. What was the old saying? A clean break heals more quickly? She had to leave the ranch before the wounds they would inflict on each other began to fester into gaping sores that would never mend.

Never far from her thoughts, *Man of Glory* stood untouched in the far corner of the studio. She couldn't work on it without being reminded of the man who had inspired it, so she'd covered it the same day he'd left for Denver and hadn't gone near it since. After she returned to New York and broke off her affair with him, then she'd be able to take it out and finish it. There was still plenty of time before the Bernard-Wilcox show, and she was still certain that her abstract depiction of man's perfection would be her most definitive work, the complete massing of her innermost thoughts, feelings and creative talents. She knew that once away from the ranch, she'd be able to call upon the well-developed resources she had to withstand the pain that would be involved in finishing the piece.

Without his customary knock, Clayton walked into the studio before she could place the drapes over his birthday present. "You wanted to see me, Lys?"

He stopped in midstride when he spied the gleaming stallion rearing up on its white quartz base. His throat worked but no words came as he walked slowly toward the sculpted figure and reached out to touch it. "Oh, Lysandra! It goes far beyond the first." He stroked the arching neck, his eyes going soft as if recalling the animal reborn in the piece.

"I didn't think when I walked in," he apologized, but his pleasure was far too evident for her to take offense at his untimely arrival. "Look at how marvelously you've captured his aggression. That's Hurricane all right, a savage brute whose graceful strides could catch the wind."

Unable to chastise him, Lysandra stood away from the worktable. "I'm glad you like it, Clayton."

"Like it!" He bounded toward her and wrapped his arms around her, lifting her feet off the ground as he whirled her in a wide circle. "It's perfect!"

They enthused over the golden stallion for a few more minutes before Lysandra broached the subject that had fostered their meeting. "Clayton, I . . . I need to ask you a favor."

Gathering all her courage, she told him exactly

why she had to leave. Of course, he did his best to talk her out of going and was almost as magnetically persuasive as his son, but she remained adamant. She didn't see the disappointment or disapproval that she had expected her request to evoke in him and sensed that Clayton had always half-known she wouldn't be able to live under the conditions his son had set down. When at long last he was convinced that she wouldn't change her mind and that it was the only course left open to her, Clayton did everything in his power to smooth the way for her as she got ready to leave.

Their parting was as emotionally draining as she had anticipated, and by the next morning when the Honours' private jet was winging its way across the lofty Rocky Mountains to New York, Lysandra felt as if a piece of her heart had been torn out of her body, leaving her drained of all feeling. Even though Clayton's last words to her had been his promise to always remain her friend, she knew that she'd never see him again.

Back in New York, her apartment seemed cold, no longer the safe haven she had created for herself. It was almost a week before she lost her fear that Adam might follow her. Eventually, she decided that leaving him in much the same way his mother had done years before had probably killed any affection he might have felt for her.

She informed Sonja of her return but refused to disclose more than the sketchiest information about her work for the Honours, dwelling mainly on Clayton's appreciation of the bronze version of Hurricane.

By the end of the month, she was close to completing the final chasing on *Man of Glory*, aware that she was about to present to the world the naked essence of her most intimate feelings. Knowing she'd need someone to lean on, she accepted Todd Bertrum's kind invitation to escort her to the showing.

The night of the show, she dressed in a simple gown of white crêpe de chine. Its Grecian style left one shoulder bare; the soft, fluid fabric draped across her full breasts then fell simply to the floor. She pulled her long hair up into a tight bun at the crown of her head; small black wisps were curled to frame her face and added to the classic elegance of her appearance. A hammered gold choker and arm bracelet enhanced the Grecian look, the warm gold relieving the stark white of her gown.

Todd's smiling brown eyes approved her appearance as he stood by the front door of her apartment and placed her fringed silk shawl over her bare shoulders. They chatted amiably during the taxi ride to the Bernard-Wilcox Gallery and kept up the pleasant conversation while Todd escorted her through the crowd of elegantly dressed men and women who jammed the immense glass-enclosed foyer of the modern building.

In a few minutes, they were mingling with the other guests who had also received gold-embossed invitations to the gala event undertaken each year to promote the country's newest aspirants to the coveted Homer Bernard Award for excellence.

"Nervous?" Todd smiled into her unnaturally drawn features, offering her a glass of champagne. Lysandra nodded, gladly accepting the glass and taking a sip as she scanned the milling clusters of people who were passing from one display to the next. She didn't dare count the people who stood before *Man of Glory,* and she breathlessly asked Todd if it appeared as if her work was fostering much interest.

"I think you're a winner." Todd glanced toward her piece. "There are at least two judges standing over there, and they look intrigued."

Rather than elating her, the information made her even more nervous. The judges would announce their decisions during the opening ceremony, eliminating the anxiety of the nervous competitors before too much of the evening had elapsed.

Shivers of apprehension raced up her spine when the silver-haired owner of the gallery, Jerome Wilcox, a strong voice and a respected opinion in the arts, stepped across to the raised platform at one side of the room and asked for everyone's attention.

Wilcox introduced the judges seated in a row behind him, who acknowledged the gathered crowd with small nods of their heads. Lysandra's fingernails dug into the soft skin of her palms as the art critic for the *New York Times* stood up to inform them who had won the first award. A round of applause greeted each name as the different judges read the various categories and awards. Finally, all that re-mained was the Bernard Award.

Once again Lysandra's work had been ignored by the critics. She felt a sharp pang of disappointment that she firmly quelled but accepted the sympathetic clasp of Todd's hand. They waited with the others for Wilcox to present the final award of the evening.

"Ladies and gentlemen, as you know, Homer Bernard appreciated art as the most truthful form of human expression," Wilcox announced grandly. "Tonight, I'm happy to bestow on a most talented newcomer to this exhibition the Homer Bernard Award. L. Scott Dillinger has created a unique blend of the abstract and the real in her ingenious sculpture entitled *Man of Glory*. We are proud to bestow our highest honor on a piece that marvelously brings together the modern elements of avant-garde with the traditional principles from which all fine art has evolved."

Only Todd's firm hand at her back enabled Ly-sandra to move. Stunned by the tribute and aston-ished at the spontaneity of the crowd's thundering applause, she felt as if the world had suddenly moved into slow motion. Somehow she reached the carpeted platform and was immediately surrounded by gracious well-wishers as she was ushered to Jerome Wilcox's side.

The elderly man took her hand and bent forward to kiss her lightly on the cheek as he offered her his personal congratulations. She wasn't able to do much more than utter a heartfelt thank you to the judges, the gallery and the guests before she was surrounded by a crowd of photographers, critics and reporters who represented the vast multitude of publications covering the event.

"You've done it, Lys," Todd applauded as soon as they were able to find a short moment together later on in the evening.

"I'm still in a state of shock." Elated, yet emotionally drained, Lysandra leaned back against one of the white pillars that surrounded the gallery's central atrium. "I'd hoped that *Man of Glory* would attract some kind of interest, but I never expected them to give it the Bernard. It's not as progressive as the past works that have won."

"You deserved it, Lys," Todd said firmly, taking her elbow as he shouldered his way past a group of people who blocked the stone walkway beside them. "Would you like to sit down for a minute? I spotted a vacant bench in the center of that mass of greenery they've planted in here."

Gazing at the cool expanse of foliage, Lysandra wistfully declined. "I have several people waiting for me at the display. I'm afraid I should get over there and tell everyone once and for all that *Man of Glory* isn't for sale."

"Not at any price, Ms. Dillinger?" The low static question was delivered by a voice she'd thought she'd never hear again. Whirling around, Lysandra saw Adam leaning against the next pillar, the white marble a perfect foil for his black evening clothes. His negligent pose belied the suppressed violence in his untamed eyes, now fixed on the paralyzed features of her face. With the fluid grace of a leashed panther, he propelled himself away from the pillar, the unrelieved white of his shirt front exposed as he slipped both hands into the pockets of his dark trousers.

Wanting to run but rooted to the spot, Lysandra stared at him, drinking in the arrogant features that were never far from her thoughts and always in her dreams. His silver-gold hair was brushed to a metallic sheen that reflected the glistening lights from the overhead chandeliers.

The inspiration for *Man of Glory* was undeniably real and standing before her. He was also intent on confronting her with everything that she had forced to the hithermost recesses of her mind. Every movement of his long-limbed body provoked an unbidden response from deep within her.

Some inner radar tuned her into the disturbing intensity of his gaze. It was as though the slightest misstep on her part would detonate the explosive emotions that were barely held in check, residing only slightly beneath the urbane exterior he presented to Todd.

Swallowing the fear that turned her mouth to cotton, she watched him shake Todd's hand. In a measured tone that intimated far more than was contained in his polite words, Adam told Todd that he needed to speak privately with Lysandra.

Todd was not a small man, but his rather hasty withdrawal demonstrated that she was not alone in her estimation of Adam's challenging mood. In a matter of seconds, Adam had managed to send Todd away without his asking a single question or inquiring whether or not she wished to be left alone with the aggressive intruder.

Sensing danger, Lysandra took a cowardly step in the direction of Todd's retreating form, but she wasn't allowed to move an inch before Adam's scorching fingers descended on her arm. "Did you have a wrap?" he asked, a grim smile hardening his mouth.

"What are you doing here, Adam?" Lysandra managed to breathe, the feel of his fingers on her arm making the blood pound in her chest. She didn't know if his movement was deliberate, but she was immediately intimidated by his height, and she quailed at the forbidding shadow of his dark form.

"Don't you think I've a right to be here, Lys?" He began moving them toward the crush of people who stood admiring *Man of Glory*. "Congratulations. I didn't believe you when you told me no one would recognize me, or that I'd be proud of being part of that piece, but you were right. I've been here for almost an hour, and all I've heard is how deserving you are of the Bernard Award." The congenial words were swiftly marred by his next statement. "Only you and I are aware of what else you deserve, aren't we?"

Her breath was coming in rapid gasps by the time they had skirted the cocktail bar and reached the crowd that stood in front of her sculpture.

"Why are you doing this?" she demanded but was immediately recognized, and several people stepped forward to ask if she planned to sell *Man of Glory*.

Before she could open her mouth to say anything, Adam spoke for her, infuriating her with the tight clasp he had taken about her waist and confusing her by the entrancing sparkle in his devastating bedroom eyes.

"As the model for this amazing piece," Adam dropped a light kiss on the top of Lysandra's head, "I think I should have first chance of buying it. That is if Ms. Dillinger is offering it for sale. Don't you think so?"

Adam's question instigated a renewed surge of interest in the bronze form that graced the pedestal. The crowd now looked at him through new eyes, but rather than showing any embarrassment at their vigorous inspection of his physique, Adam seemed to take it all in his stride. His eyes were amused as he watched the rapid comparisons being made between his muscular frame and the symmetrical nude she had portrayed in her work.

Lysandra was shocked speechless, open-mouthed, as he relayed to the fascinated audience how he felt about being the model for the piece they all admired.

"No wonder *Man of Glory* is so remarkably animated," a matronly-looking woman in a luxurious ermine stole gushed.

"Looking at the two of you together, now we know what inspired this marvelous piece," another piped in and cast a knowing glance at Lysandra. "It's a work of love, my dear, and there's no greater challenge than that, is there?"

"Not that I've found," Adam cut in, agreeing with

the others that Lysandra had given herself wholly to her work but implying it was because she had already given herself body and soul to the man.

"Stop it!" Lysandra ordered desperately under her breath, hiding her temper behind a wide insincere smile. She was fast discovering exactly what Adam thought she deserved and wanted to scream as he drew her with him through the curious crowd of onlookers. By the time he announced that they had to leave, he'd made sure that everyone was aware of his part in the work that had achieved such critical acclaim.

Thoroughly exasperated, she was more than willing to go—anything to escape the knowing comments and inquisitive eyes that followed them wherever they went.

12

~~~~~~~~~~

How dare you!" Lysandra cried once they were safely ensconced in a taxi and riding back to her apartment. "I came with Todd. I should have left with him, but you made it seem as if you're the only man in my life."

His short laugh did nothing to alleviate her frustration, and she didn't heed the warning glance he threw her as he settled himself more comfortably on the seat, lifting his arm across the upholstered back until his hand lay scant inches from her nape. The fine hairs prickled at his nearness, but she was too angry to respond to the delicious sensation. She attempted to slide across the seat and put a greater distance between them, but his fingers quickly clamped around her neck, roughly tangling in the upswept strands of her hair.

"I'm the only man in your life who has the right to do this," Adam retorted in the sensually low drawl that made her nerves scream with awareness. He forced her chin up, and his head swooped down.

His mouth was both a brand and a balm, marking her lips and medicating her resistance with the thrust of his tongue. Her whimpered protests became the moans of longing he'd always been able to inspire in her, and the triumphant glitter in his eyes when he released her told her that he was well aware of the effect he still had on her.

She resorted to a speaking silence, holding herself with both arms to prevent the trembling that was spreading through her body. It didn't seem to bother him in the least that she was neither looking nor speaking to him. He turned away from her and gazed out through the window, his interest seemingly centered on the passing buildings.

Given his profile, Lysandra couldn't help her gaze from straying to the bold lines of his face, outlining the strong jaw and wide brow as if memorizing every facet she had been deprived of seeing for so long, despaired of seeing ever again.

When they pulled up in front of her building, he paid the driver, then asked for her key, brooking no argument, and ushered them both up the stairs to her apartment. Once inside, Lysandra walked across the room and turned on the lights, her flaring eyes the only sign that she was not totally resigned to whatever was coming.

Adam watched her closely as she removed her wrap from her slender shoulders and threw it across her bed, his glance narrowing on the amount of bare skin exposed at the back of her gown. She swung around to face him, her cameo face high with color, her dark eyes huge as she lifted her chin like a prizefighter confronted with a less than worthy opponent. He had to admire her spirit and couldn't prevent the slow smile that spread across his face before he uttered the verbal blow that would have been called a foul if they'd been in the ring.

"It's unfortunate that you're looking twice as beautiful as I remembered." He sauntered across the room and sat down in one of the rattan chairs that were grouped around the oriental carpet. "It makes it difficult for me to say what needs to be said, when all I want to do is undrape those virginal white folds."

Lysandra's legs wouldn't hold her, and she sank into the nearest chair, unconsciously encouraging further conversation by taking a seat.

"I've missed you, Lys, and by your response to me in the taxi, it looks as if you still recall who it is you belong to."

Shocked by his unfair method of attack, Lysandra sat transfixed, unable to think of anything insulting enough to say. Then she noticed the tenseness of his body when he stretched out his legs. Was it possible that he didn't feel as confident as his words implied? She was unable to make her lips form a coherent sound, but her brain engaged and she looked at him closely.

There were several new lines around his sensual mouth, an unnatural pallor beneath his healthy tan, and he had taken an overtight grip on the arms of the chair, his knuckles white as he attempted to maintain his bold expression.

"Why are you here, Adam?" Lysandra repeated, half-dreading what he'd say now that they were alone and no one else could hear his answer.

"I'm here to find out why you walked out on me." Adam seemed inordinately interested in the toes of his shoes. "I never thought you'd do that to me, Lys. I'm wondering if you were lying to me when you said you loved me. Perhaps all you wanted was a cooperative model for that award-winning piece you exhibited tonight. Was that what you had in mind when I made love to you? Did you take artistic notes every time you touched me?"

It was not in her imagination. Adam's harsh words were tinged with pain and bitterness. He swallowed convulsively, as if the words had burned in his throat.

It took only an instant for the agony in his tone to tear down the dam she'd erected since he'd kissed her. "I did love you, Adam. I . . . I've never stopped, but I couldn't stay knowing that all the feeling was on my side."

She bowed her head. "Clayton told me about your mother. I didn't want to leave you the same way she did, but you didn't give me any choice. If I had become your mistress, it would have destroyed us. I'm not able to take what I want without accepting the responsibility that needs to go with it."

Staring at her clasped hands, her voice cracked with misery. "I knew that if I waited for you and told

175

you how I felt, you'd be able to change my mind. You needn't think I've been able to forget what I did. I knew I'd be hurting you, but I thought it best to get it over with and not wait until we had a far more painful breakup later on."

"I see." Adam's voice broke on the words, and she lifted her head to see him staring at her, his guilt-ridden expression making him look almost haggard. "I've got a lot to learn about loving, Lys. My father told me how it was for you, but like a fool, I didn't listen and wouldn't believe him. I was too damned angry with you for leaving me."

As if it pained him to see her face, he brushed his hand over his eyes, then bent over, resting his elbows on his knees and locking his hands together as he stared at the floor. "You've got what you want. Over the past few weeks, I've learned that I'll take you on any terms. Tonight you said you wouldn't sell *Man of Glory* for any price. Would you buy the model if the tag read marriage?"

It was the defeated slump to his shoulders that made her say, "No, Adam. I can't."

The tears that had been threatening all night began to fall, rolling down her cheeks in silent trickles. She sensed that he had risen to his feet, preparing to go, but she had to make sure he fully understood why his proposal wasn't accepted.

"Don't you understand?" she asked, sobbing. "I love you too much to force that on you. All I ask is that you forgive me for not having the courage to tell you how I felt about marriage."

Overwhelming despair swept through her body as she talked, the words barely decipherable. "I couldn't stand to live with you and not look forward to the day when we'd have children. If I loved a man, I'd want his children more than anything else in the world, but I know your feelings on the subject. If you ever agreed to let me get pregnant, our child would sense he wasn't wanted by both parents. I'm sorry, but I couldn't stand that." Her sobbing increased. "I'm so sorry. . . ."

She felt herself being lifted from the chair but couldn't believe that it was Adam's arms that held her or Adam's voice that was washing over her, his heartrending pleas for forgiveness attempting to assuage her weeping. She blinked her eyes, staring at him through the wet veil of her lashes and couldn't comprehend that his proud features were twisted by self-recrimination.

"God, Lys. Don't go on like this. I can't stand it. I love you so." His jumbled, nearly incoherent phrases ran together, the pain in his eyes hurting her. "I'll make it up to you, my love," he vowed, "I promise. We'll have dozens of children."

"Adam?" Her fingers stroked behind his neck, compassion drying her tears. She brought his blond head down to rest against her damp cheek. "Adam, are you saying that you *want* to marry me? For yourself? Not just for me?"

A dazed expression came into his eyes, and in seconds he had settled them both in one chair. Adjusting her on his lap, caressing her hair and kissing her cheeks, her eyes, the tip of her nose, he treated her as if she were the most precious thing in the world.

"I love you, Lys," Adam declared gruffly, "and it's the kind of love that requires marriage and a permanent home. Our children will never doubt that they aren't loved by both parents. Tell me you'll marry me for I won't accept anything less than a total commitment."

Twisting in his lap, her arms stretched up to cling around his neck as she gave him her soft mouth. The kiss was intense, proving the depth of her love and joining their souls with the eternal bonds that had ensnared men and women since the beginning of time.

"I need to be your wife, Adam," Lysandra whispered huskily, her fingers trembling across the brown column of his throat as she abated the hunger that had gripped her since their parting. "I've been yours since the first night, and I'll be yours forever."

"I missed you so much I thought I'd go insane," he whispered huskily, grabbing her fingers and kissing each one of them in turn. "I was afraid that you were only using me. I realized that even that would be better than the emptiness I felt without you. My dad waited for me to hit rock bottom before he began to pick up the pieces and attempted to pound some sense into my thick head."

He took a deep breath, then gave a sigh of relief and rueful surrender. "Tonight, when I saw you with Bertrum, all my doubts came back. You'd never looked more beautiful, and it wasn't for me."

"Todd has been a good friend." She wiggled closer, pressing her cheek to his dark jacket. "He knew that I was involved with someone else, and tonight you made it clear who that someone was."

His chuckle was most unapologetic. "So I did." He slid his arm around her waist and gave her a tender squeeze. "I need to explain something to you, Lys. Stop distracting me."

"Whatever you say." Lysandra reveled in the thought that the feel of her legs shifting for a more comfortable position on his lap could destroy his concentration.

"When Dad and I finally talked, I realized why my mother did what she did. Dad was able to forgive her, but I wasn't. Now I understand why it was impossible for you to tell me you were leaving. You loved me too much to see me hurt just as my mother did all those years ago. It's still painful for me to think about her, but I've grown up enough to hope she found some kind of happiness with her second husband."

For the first time, Lysandra saw a hint of compassion in Adam's eyes as he talked about his mother. "She knew I was part of that ranch and couldn't separate me from what's in my blood, any more than she could cut herself off from her roots. She had to go, and had to leave me and Dad behind."

Lysandra could feel the tension drain out of him and knew she'd never again see the cynicism in him that used to frighten her so much. Adam had managed to overcome the stumbling block that had stunted his ability to give all of himself to another person. The Adam who asked her to become his wife was a man who had come to grips with his past.

Lysandra appreciated how much they had each grown since the day they had met. Both of them would benefit from the painful maturation that would now bring them closer together instead of driving them apart.

"I'm glad you feel that way about her, Adam," Lysandra said sincerely, then put a stop to the conversation by beginning to unbutton his shirt. When that task was complete, she reached up and started tugging on the satin ends of his black tie. The slippery material was drawn from beneath the starched collar of his shirt, and she dropped it onto the floor.

"What do you think you're doing?" Adam growled, looking down at the expanse of his bare chest where she had pulled open his shirt.

"You once accused me of constantly undressing you with my eyes." Lysandra looked straight into his face so that he could see the strength of her desire. "But I'd rather undress you by hand."

She gasped when he stood up in one powerful surge of motion. "The feeling's mutual, my love."

He carried her to the bed and lay her down on the spread, first pulling the pins from her hair, then spreading the black silky strands across the pillow. "As my wife, I want you to look like this every morning when I wake up next to you." He paused, his warm blue gaze traveling leisurely down her body, then back up again. "Except for this formal gown."

He leaned down and began easing the white crêpe gown from her shoulders, his eyes never leaving her face.

"Every day," she promised, and opened her arms.

13

Lysandra carried the large cake covered with glowing candles into the dining room. "Marilee's the only one singing," she said, smiling at the little girl who was clapping her hands and enthusiastically singing "Happy Birthday" at the top of her lungs. At Lysandra's urging, the rest of the family joined their voices with the six-year-old child's.

When the boisterous, off-key singing died down and Clayton had dutifully blown out the candles, he beamed warmly at those gathered around the large table. "This has been the best day I've had in years. When you get to be my age, the only thing you want for your birthday is to be surrounded by the people you love." He turned to his daughter and son-in-law. "Sharon, Mark, it sure was a surprise when you flew in this morning."

"Dad, you know we'd never miss an occasion like this." Sharon took hold of her husband's hand and shared a conspiratorial grin with him. "Besides, we have an announcement we wanted to make in person. You're going to have to find space on your other knee next year, Dad. The Johnson family is expanding."

While everyone congratulated Sharon and Mark, Lysandra stole a glance at her husband. As she'd expected, Adam was watching her, a question in his eyes and a wide grin on his face. Like so many married couples, words were often unnecessary, and Lysandra's expression told him she wanted to wait just a while longer before they made their own announcement. This moment was for Sharon and Mark.

She couldn't prevent the small laugh that escaped through her lips at Adam's boyishly pleading expression, the impatient shifting of his broad shoulders. Stubbornly, she frowned at him, shaking her head when he got up from his chair and rounded the table. He came to stand behind her, placing both hands on her shoulders, and she could sense he was anxious for Clayton to settle down after Sharon's announcement.

Even after almost a year of marriage, Lysandra was astonished at the changes in Adam. Secure in her love, he no longer feared giving of himself, proving over and over again that he was committed body and soul to their marriage. Sharon and Clayton had each taken Lysandra aside to express their happiness at having her as part of the family and their gratitude that she had been able to bring out the best in Adam. They gave her the credit for his finally being able to forgive his mother and to open himself up. There was a deeper warmth in the affection he displayed toward all those around him; his smiles were more genuine and his bitterness was gone.

For Lysandra, their marriage provided the security of a family that she'd always craved. To her surprise, there was more. Finding herself completely loved and wanted for the first time, she'd been able to free the pent-up emotions that had lain dormant and open herself fully to the Honour family. Able to draw on those feelings, her work had improved, showing sides of herself she'd always kept hidden, the passion she'd once been afraid to display.

"It's our turn, honey," Adam whispered in her ear, drawing her up from the chair to stand beside him. He slipped his arm about her waist and held her tenderly against his side. "Can I get a word in here, folks?" he began.

"There's a call for you, Lysandra," Betty interrupted from the doorway. "It's that nice Mrs. Parker from New York."

Looking up into her husband's face, Lysandra giggled at his annoyed scowl. "I'll be right back," she promised, having difficulty breaking his hold on her.

"Can't you return the call later?" Adam implored. "After all, we'll be in New York day after tomorrow. What can Sonja have to say that won't wait?"

"It must be important, Adam," Lysandra insisted, edging away.

Sharon handed Adam a plate holding a large piece

of birthday cake. "This ought to hold you 'til your bride gets back." She grinned good-naturedly and shooed her sister-in-law out of the room. "Sonja probably couldn't wait until tomorrow to tell Lys how good her new work is. You know her, Adam. I bet she's got Lys booked to meet every gallery owner in New York."

"I hope not," Adam growled. "I wanted to spend a few days alone with her."

"Are you kidding?" Sharon hooted. "You've done nothing else since you two were married. I bet Dad hardly ever sees her. I had to kidnap her last month in order to go shopping in Denver."

"We'd have been better off if they'd actually been kidnapped," Mark interjected. "According to my checkbook, a ransom would have been cheaper. I don't blame you for keeping Lys away from Sharon. If anyone knows how to spend money, it's her."

"Always did," Clayton joked. "Why do you suppose I married her off so young?"

By the time Lysandra had completed her conversation with Sonja, the rest of the family was engrossed in unrestrained teasing, each of the various family members taking it as fast as they were dishing it out. Hesitating in the doorway, Lysandra listened to the familial interchanges, knowing if she stepped into the room she'd immediately be swept into the fray. It had taken her a while to feel comfortable taking part in the affectionate razzing that took place, but now she cherished those times and knew they signified belonging.

"Sonja's throwing a party for us after the show,"

Lysandra informed them as she walked into the room, and was about to continue when Adam interrupted firmly.

"Before we get off on another subject," Adam said and included both his wife and sister in his pointed stare, "I'd like to request a moment of sobriety. Since the major stockholders of the Honour Corporation are present, I think this is the best time to discuss adding a new member to the board."

"I don't believe it." Sharon groaned. "Even on Dad's birthday you have to talk business."

Clayton leaned forward, curiosity and concern wiping the smile from his face. "Why haven't you discussed this with me before?"

Adam's lips twitched. "Because you weren't involved in the negotiations," he said firmly, his blue eyes twinkling.

"Adam," Lysandra admonished, feeling a blush come up on her cheeks.

Giving her a sheepish grin, Adam didn't delay any longer. "In seven months or so, there'll be another Honour joining the family." Pulling Lysandra under his arm, he let all the pride he was feeling show in his smile. "Lys and I are expecting a baby."

For a few minutes, total silence greeted the announcement, then everyone began to talk at once. "This is great news," Sharon enthused. "I can feel another shopping spree coming on." She wasn't allowed to continue as Mark moved his chair next to hers and placed a silencing finger over her lips, nodding to her father whose face was lit with joy.

"What do you think of that, Marilee?" Clayton

gently lowered the little girl from his lap but kept hold of her hand. "You're getting a little brother or sister and a new cousin, too."

Seeing the tears in her father's eyes, Sharon discreetly motioned her daughter to her chair. Clayton walked over to Adam and Lysandra and wrapped his arms around both of them. "You don't know what I'm feelin'," he murmured huskily.

But Lysandra did. She was glad to be a part of the future, a future that would bring another proud generation to the mountains of Colorado.

Silhouette Desire
15-Day Trial Offer
A new romance series that explores contemporary relationships in exciting detail

Six Silhouette Desire romances, free for 15 days!
We'll send you six new Silhouette Desire romances
to look over for 15 days, absolutely free! If you decide
not to keep the books, return them and owe nothing.

Six books a month, free home delivery. If you like
Silhouette Desire romances as much as we think you
will, keep them and return your payment with the
invoice. Then we will send you six new books every
month to preview, just as soon as they are published.
You pay only for the books you decide to keep, and
you never pay postage and handling.

Silhouette Desire

YOU'LL BE SWEPT AWAY WITH SILHOUETTE DESIRE

$1.75 each

1 ☐ James
2 ☐ Monet
3 ☐ Clay
4 ☐ Carey

5 ☐ Baker
6 ☐ Mallory
7 ☐ St. Claire

8 ☐ Dee
9 ☐ Simms
10 ☐ Smith

$1.95 each

11 ☐ James
12 ☐ Palmer
13 ☐ Wallace
14 ☐ Valley
15 ☐ Vernon
16 ☐ Major
17 ☐ Simms
18 ☐ Ross
19 ☐ James
20 ☐ Allison
21 ☐ Baker
22 ☐ Durant
23 ☐ Sunshine
24 ☐ Baxter
25 ☐ James
26 ☐ Palmer
27 ☐ Conrad
28 ☐ Lovan

29 ☐ Michelle
30 ☐ Lind
31 ☐ James
32 ☐ Clay
33 ☐ Powers
34 ☐ Milan
35 ☐ Major
36 ☐ Summers
37 ☐ James
38 ☐ Douglass
39 ☐ Monet
40 ☐ Mallory
41 ☐ St. Claire
42 ☐ Stewart
43 ☐ Simms
44 ☐ West
45 ☐ Clay
46 ☐ Chance

47 ☐ Michelle
48 ☐ Powers
49 ☐ James
50 ☐ Palmer
51 ☐ Lind
52 ☐ Morgan
53 ☐ Joyce
54 ☐ Fulford
55 ☐ James
56 ☐ Douglass
57 ☐ Michelle
58 ☐ Mallory
59 ☐ Powers
60 ☐ Dennis
61 ☐ Simms
62 ☐ Monet
63 ☐ Dee
64 ☐ Milan

65 ☐ Allison
66 ☐ Langtry
67 ☐ James
68 ☐ Browning
69 ☐ Carey
70 ☐ Victor
71 ☐ Joyce
72 ☐ Hart
73 ☐ St. Clair
74 ☐ Douglass
75 ☐ McKenna
76 ☐ Michelle
77 ☐ Lowell
78 ☐ Barber
79 ☐ Simms
80 ☐ Palmer
81 ☐ Kennedy
82 ☐ Clay

YOU'LL BE SWEPT AWAY WITH SILHOUETTE DESIRE

$1.95 each

83 ☐ Chance	88 ☐ Trevor	93 ☐ Berk	98 ☐ Joyce
84 ☐ Powers	89 ☐ Ross	94 ☐ Robbins	99 ☐ Major
85 ☐ James	90 ☐ Roszel	95 ☐ Summers	100 ☐ Howard
86 ☐ Malek	91 ☐ Browning	96 ☐ Milan	101 ☐ Morgan
87 ☐ Michelle	92 ☐ Carey	97 ☐ James	102 ☐ Palmer